$5.45

Master
of
the World

Jules Verne

A WATERMILL CLASSIC

Contents of this edition copyright © 1985 by Watermill Press, Mahwah, New Jersey.

Printed in the United States of America.

ISBN 0-8167-0459-7

Chapter 1

What Happened in the Mountains

If I speak of myself in this story, it is because I have been deeply involved in its startling events, events doubtless among the most extraordinary which this twentieth century will witness. Sometimes I even ask myself if all this has really happened, if its pictures dwell in truth in my memory, and not merely in my imagination. In my position as head inspector in the federal police department at Washington, urged on moreover by the desire, which has always been very strong in me, to investigate and understand everything which is mysterious, I naturally became much interested in these remarkable occurrences. And as I have been employed by the government in various important affairs and secret missions since I was a mere lad, it also happened very naturally that the head of my department placed in my charge this astonishing investigation, wherein I found myself wrestling with so many impenetrable mysteries.

In the remarkable passages of the recital, it is important that you should believe my word. For some of the facts I can bring no other testimony than my own. If you do not wish to believe me, so be it. I can scarce believe it all myself.

The strange occurrences began in the western part of our great American state of North Carolina. There, deep amid the Blue Ridge Mountains rises the crest called the Great Eyrie. Its huge rounded form is distinctly seen from the little town of Morganton on the Catawba River, and still more clearly as one approaches the mountains by way of the village of Pleasant Garden.

Why the name of Great Eyrie was originally given this mountain by the people of the surrounding region, I am not quite sure. It rises rocky and grim and inaccessible, and under certain atmospheric conditions has a peculiarly blue and distant effect. But the idea one would naturally get from the name is of a refuge for birds of prey, eagles, condors, vultures; the home of vast numbers of the feathered tribes, wheeling and screaming above the peaks beyond the reach of man. Now, the Great Eyrie did not seem particularly attractive to birds; on the contrary, the people of the neighborhood began to remark that on some days when birds approached its summit they mounted still further, circled high above the crest, and then flew swiftly away, troubling the air with harsh cries.

Why then the name Great Eyrie? Perhaps the mount might better have been called a crater, for in the center of those steep and rounded walls there might well be a huge deep basin. Perhaps there might even lie within their circuit a mountain lake, such as exists in other parts of the Appalachian mountain system, a lagoon fed by the rain and the winter snows.

In brief was not this the site of an ancient volcano, one which had slept through ages, but whose inner fires might yet reawake? Might not the Great Eyrie reproduce in its neighborhood the violence of Mount Krakatoa or the terrible disaster of Mount Pelée? If there were indeed a central lake, was there not danger that its waters, penetrating the strata beneath, would be turned to steam by the volcanic fires and tear their way forth in a tremendous explosion, deluging the fair plains of Carolina with an eruption such as that of 1902 in Martinique?

Indeed, with regard to this last possibility there had been certain symptoms recently observed which might well be due to volcanic action. Smoke had floated above the mountain and once the country folk passing near had heard subterranean noises, unexplainable rumblings. A glow in the sky had crowned the height at night.

When the wind blew the smoky cloud eastward toward Pleasant Garden, a few cinders and ashes drifted down from it. And finally one stormy night pale flames, reflected from the clouds above the summit, cast upon the district below a sinister, warning light.

In presence of these strange phenomena, it is not astonishing that the people of the surrounding district became seriously disquieted.

And to the disquiet was joined an imperious need of knowing the true condition of the mountain. The Carolina newspapers had flaring headlines, "The Mystery of the Great Eyrie!" They asked if it was not dangerous to dwell in such a region. Their articles aroused curiosity and fear—curiosity among those who being in no danger themselves were interested in the disturbance merely as a strange phenomenon of nature, fear in those who were likely to be the victims if a catastrophe actually occurred. Those more immediately threatened were the citizens of Morganton, and even more the good folk of Pleasant Garden and the hamlets and farms yet closer to the mountain.

Assuredly it was regrettable that mountain climbers had not previously attempted to ascend to the summit of the Great Eyrie. The cliffs of rock which surrounded it had never been scaled. Perhaps they might offer no path by which even the most daring climber could penetrate to the interior. Yet, if a volcanic eruption menaced all the western region of the Carolinas, then a complete examination of the mountain was become absolutely necessary.

Now before the actual ascent of the crater, with its many serious difficulties, was attempted, there was one way which offered an opportunity of reconnoitering the interior, without clambering up the precipices. In the first days of September of that memorable year, a well-known aeronaut named Wilker came to Morganton, with his balloon. By waiting for a breeze from the east, he could easily rise in his balloon and drift over the Great Eyrie. There from a safe height above he could search with a powerful glass into its deeps. Thus he would know if the mouth of a volcano really opened amid the mighty rocks. This was the principal question. If this were settled, it would be known if the surrounding country must fear an eruption at some period more or less distant.

The ascension was begun according to the program suggested. The wind was fair and steady; the sky clear; the morning clouds were disappearing under the vigorous rays of the sun. If the interior of the Great Eyrie was not filled with smoke, the aeronaut would be able to search with his glass its entire extent. If the vapors were rising, he, no doubt, could detect their source.

The balloon rose at once to a height of fifteen hundred feet, and there rested almost motionless for a quarter of an hour. Evidently the east wind, which was brisk upon the surface of the earth, did not make itself felt at that height. Then, unlucky chance, the balloon was caught in an adverse current, and began to drift toward the east. Its distance from the mountain chain rapidly increased. Despite all the efforts of the aeronaut, the citizens of Morganton saw the balloon disappear on the wrong horizon. Later, they learned that it had landed in the neighborhood of Raleigh, the capital of North Carolina.

This attempt having failed, it was agreed that it should be tried again under better conditions. Indeed, fresh rumblings were heard from the mountain, accompanied by heavy clouds and wavering glimmerings of light at night. Folk began to realize that the Great Eyrie was a serious and perhaps imminent source of danger. Yes, the entire country lay under the threat of some seismic or volcanic disaster.

During the first days of April of that year, these more or less vague apprehensions turned to actual panic. The newspapers gave prompt echo to the public terror. The entire district between the mountains and Morganton was sure that an eruption was at hand.

The night of the fourth of April, the good folk of Pleasant Garden were awakened by a sudden uproar. They thought that the mountains were falling upon them. They rushed from their houses, ready for instant flight, fearing to see open before them some immense abyss, engulfing the farms and villages for miles around.

The night was very dark. A weight of heavy clouds pressed down upon the plain. Even had it been day the crest of the mountains would have been invisible.

In the midst of this impenetrable obscurity, there was no response to the cries which arose from every side. Frightened groups of men, women, and children groped their way along the black roads in wild confusion. From every quarter came the screaming voices: "It is an earthquake!" "It is an eruption!" "Whence comes it?" "From the Great Eyrie!"

Into Morganton sped the news that stones, lava, ashes, were raining down upon the country.

Shrewd citizens of the town, however, observed that if there were an eruption the noise would have continued and increased, the flames would have appeared above the crater; or at least their lurid reflections would have penetrated the clouds. Now, even these reflections were no longer seen. If there had been an earthquake, the terrified people saw that at least their houses had not crumbled beneath the shock. It was possible that the uproar had been caused by an avalanche, the fall of some mighty rock from the summit of the mountains.

An hour passed without other incident. A wind from the west sweeping over the long chain of the Blue Ridge, set the pines and hemlocks wailing on the higher slopes. There seemed no new cause for panic; and folk began to return to their houses. All, however, awaited impatiently the return of day.

Then suddenly, toward three o'clock in the morning, another alarm! Flames leaped up above the rocky wall of the Great Eyrie. Reflected from the clouds, they illuminated the atmosphere for a great distance. A crackling, as if of many burning trees, was heard.

Had a fire spontaneously broken out? And to what cause was it due? Lightning could not have started the conflagration; for no thunder had been heard. True, there was plenty of material for fire; at this height the chain of the Blue Ridge is well wooded. But these flames were too sudden for any ordinary cause.

"An eruption!" "An eruption!"

The cry resounded from all sides. An eruption!

The Great Eyrie was then indeed the crater of a volcano buried in the bowels of the mountains. And after so many years, so many ages even, had it reawakened? Added to the flames, was a rain of stone and ash about to follow? Were the lavas going to pour down torrents of molten fire, destroying everything in their passage, annihilating the towns, the villages, the farms, all this beautiful world of meadows, fields and forests, even as far as Pleasant Garden and Morganton?

This time the panic was overwhelming; nothing could stop it. Women carrying their infants, crazed with terror, rushed along the eastward roads. Men, deserting their homes, made hurried bundles of their most precious belongings and set free their livestock, cows, sheep, pigs, which fled in all directions. What disorder resulted from this agglomeration, human and animal, under darkest night, amid forests, threatened by the fires of the volcano, along the border of marshes whose waters might be upheaved and overflow! With the earth itself threatening to disappear from under the feet of the fugitives would they be in time to save themselves, if a cascade of glowing lava came rolling down the slope of the mountain across their route?

Nevertheless, some of the chief and shrewder farm owners were not swept away in this mad flight, which they did their best to restrain. Venturing within a mile of the mountain, they saw that the glare of the flames was decreasing. In truth it hardly seemed that the region was immediately menaced by any further upheaval.

No stones were being hurled into space; no torrent of lava was visible upon the slopes; no rumblings rose from the ground. There was no further manifestation of any seismic disturbance capable of overwhelming the land.

At length, the flight of the fugitives ceased at a distance where they seemed secure from all danger. Then a few ventured back toward the mountain. Some farms were reoccupied before the break of day.

By morning the crests of the Great Eyrie showed scarcely the least remnant of its cloud of smoke. The fires were certainly at an end; and if it were impossible to determine their cause, one might at least hope that they would not break out again.

It appeared possible that the Great Eyrie had not really been the theater of volcanic phenomena at all. There was no further evidence that the neighborhood was at the mercy either of eruptions or of earthquakes.

Yet once more about five o'clock, from beneath the ridge of the mountain, where the shadows of night still lingered, a strange noise swept across the air, a sort of whirring, accompanied by the beating of mighty wings. And had it been a clear day, perhaps the farmers would have seen the passage of a mighty bird of prey, some monster of the skies, which having risen from the Great Eyrie sped away toward the east.

Chapter 2

I Reach Morganton

The twenty-seventh of April, having left Washington the night before, I arrived at Raleigh, the capital of the State of North Carolina.

Two days before, the head of the federal police had called me to his room. He was awaiting me with some impatience. "John Strock," said he, "are you still the man who on so many occasions has proven to me both his devotion and his ability?"

"Mr. Ward," I answered, with a bow, "I cannot promise success or even ability, but as to devotion, I assure you, it is yours."

"I do not doubt it," responded the chief. "And I will ask you instead this more exact question: Are you as fond of riddles as ever? As eager to penetrate into mysteries, as I have known you before?"

"I am, Mr. Ward."

"Good, Strock; then listen."

Mr. Ward, a man of about fifty years, of great power and intellect, was fully master of the important position he filled. He had several times entrusted to me difficult missions which I had accomplished successfully, and which had won me his confidence. For several months past, however, he had found no occasion for my services. Therefore I awaited with impatience what he had to say. I did not doubt that his questioning implied a serious and important task for me.

"Doubtless you know," said he, "what has happened down in the Blue Ridge Mountains near Morganton."

"Surely, Mr. Ward, the phenomena reported from there have been singular enough to arouse anyone's curiosity."

"They are singular, even remarkable, Strock. No doubt about that. But there is also reason to ask, if these phenomena about the Great Eyrie are not a source of continued danger to the people there, if they are not forerunners of some disaster as terrible as it is mysterious."

"It is to be feared, sir."

"So we must know, Strock, what is inside of that mountain. If we are helpless in the face of some great force of nature, people must be warned in time of the danger which threatens them."

"It is clearly the duty of the authorities, Mr. Ward," responded I, "to learn what is going on within there."

"True, Strock; but that presents great difficulties. Everyone reports that it is impossible to scale the precipices of the Great Eyrie and reach its interior. But has anyone ever attempted it with scientific appliances and under the best conditions? I doubt it, and believe a resolute attempt may bring success."

"Nothing is impossible, Mr. Ward; what we face here is merely a question of expense."

"We must not regard expense when we are seeking to reassure an entire population, or to preserve it from a catastrophe. There is another suggestion I would make to you. Perhaps this Great Eyrie is not so inaccessible as is supposed. Perhaps a band of malefactors have secreted themselves there, gaining access by ways known only to themselves."

"What! You suspect that robbers—"

"Perhaps I am wrong, Strock; and these strange sights and sounds have all had natural causes. Well, that is what we have to settle, and as quickly as possible."

"I have one question to ask."

"Go ahead, Strock."

"When the Great Eyrie has been visited, when we know the source of these phenomena, if there really is a crater there and an eruption is imminent, can we avert it?"

"No, Strock; but we can estimate the extent of the danger. If some volcano in the Alleghenies threatens North Carolina with a disaster similar to that of Martinique, buried beneath the outpourings of Mount Pelée, then these people must leave their homes—"

"I hope, sir, there is no such widespread danger."

"I think not, Strock; it seems to me highly improbable that an active volcano exists in the Blue Ridge Mountain chain. Our Appalachian mountain system is nowhere volcanic in its origin. But all these events cannot be without basis. In short, Strock, we have decided to make a strict inquiry into the phenomena of the Great Eyrie, to gather all the testimony, to question the people of the towns and farms. To do this I have made choice of an agent in whom we have full confidence; and this agent is you, Strock."

"Good! I am ready, Mr. Ward," cried I, "and be sure that I shall neglect nothing to bring you full information."

"I know it, Strock, and I will add that I regard you as specially fitted for the work. You will have a splendid opportunity to exercise, and I hope to satisfy, your favorite passion of curiosity."

"As you say, sir."

"You will be free to act according to circumstances. As to expenses, if there seems reason to organize an ascension party, which will be costly, you have *carte blanche.*"

"I will act as seems best, Mr. Ward."

"Let me caution you to act with all possible discretion. The people in the vicinity are already over-excited. It will be well to move secretly. Do not mention the suspicions I have suggested to you. And above all, avoid arousing any fresh panic."

"It is understood."

"You will be accredited to the Mayor of

Morganton, who will assist you. Once more, be prudent, Strock, and acquaint no one with your mission, unless it is absolutely necessary. You have often given proofs of your intelligence and address; and this time I feel assured you will succeed."

I asked him only, "When shall I start?"

"Tomorrow."

"Tomorrow, I shall leave Washington; and the day after, I shall be at Morganton."

How little suspicion had I of what the future had in store for me!

I returned immediately to my house where I made my preparations for departure; and the next evening found me in Raleigh. There I passed the night, and in the course of the next afternoon arrived at the railroad station of Morganton.

Morganton is but a small town, built upon strata of the Jurassic period, particularly rich in coal. Its mines give it some prosperity. It also has numerous unpleasant mineral waters, so that the season there attracts many visitors. Around Morganton is a rich farming country, with broad fields of grain. It lies in the midst of swamps, covered with mosses and reeds. Evergreen forests rise high up the mountain slopes. All that the region lacks is the wells of natural gas, that invaluable natural source of power, light, and warmth, so abundant in most of the Allegheny valleys. Villages and farms are numerous up to the very borders of the mountain forests. Thus there were many thousands of people threatened if the Great Eyrie proved indeed a volcano, if the convulsions of nature extended to Pleasant Garden and to Morganton.

The mayor of Morganton, Mr. Elias Smith, was a tall man, vigorous and enterprising, forty years old or more, and of a health to defy all the doctors of the two Americas. He was a great hunter of bears and panthers, beasts which may still be found in the wild gorges and mighty forests of the Alleghenies.

Mr. Smith was himself a rich landowner, possessing several farms in the neighborhood. Even his most distant tenants received frequent visits from him. Indeed, whenever his official duties did not keep him in his so-called home at Morganton, he was exploring the surrounding country, irresistibly drawn by the instincts of the hunter.

I went at once to the house of Mr. Smith. He was expecting me, having been warned by telegram. He received me very frankly, without any formality, his pipe in his mouth, a glass of brandy on the table. A second glass was brought in by a servant, and I had to drink to my host before beginning our interview.

"Mr. Ward sent you," said he to me in a jovial tone. "Good; let us drink to Mr. Ward's health."

I clinked glasses with him, and drank in honor of the chief of police.

"And now," demanded Elias Smith, "what is worrying him?"

At this I made known to the mayor of Morganton the cause and the purpose of my mission in North Carolina. I assured him that my chief had given me full power, and would render me every assistance, financial and otherwise, to solve the riddle and relieve the neighborhood of its anxiety relative to the Great Eyrie.

Elias Smith listened to me without uttering a word, but not without several times refilling his glass and mine. While he puffed steadily at his pipe, the close attention which he gave me was beyond question. I saw his cheeks flush at times, and his eyes gleam under their bushy brows. Evidently the chief magistrate of Morganton was uneasy about Great Eyrie, and would be as eager as I to discover the cause of these phenomena.

When I had finished my communication, Elias Smith gazed at me for some moments in silence. Then he said, softly, "So at Washington they wish to know what the Great Eyrie hides within its circuit?"

"Yes, Mr. Smith."

"And you, also?"

"I do."

"So do I, Mr. Strock."

He and I were as one in our curiosity.

"You will understand," added he, knocking the cinders from his pipe, "that as a landowner, I am much interested in these stories of the Great Eyrie, and as mayor, I wish to protect my constituents."

"A double reason," I commented, "to stimulate you to discover the cause of these extraordinary occurrences! Without doubt, my dear Mr. Smith, they have appeared to you as inexplicable and as threatening as to your people."

"Inexplicable, certainly, Mr. Strock. For on

my part, I do not believe it possible that the Great Eyrie can be a volcano; the Alleghenies are nowhere of volcanic origin. I, myself, in our immediate district, have never found any geological traces of scoria, or lava, or any eruptive rock whatever. I do not think, therefore, that Morganton can possibly be threatened from such a source.''

''You really think not, Mr. Smith?''

''Certainly.''

''But these tremblings of the earth that have been felt in the neighborhood!''

''Yes, these tremblings! These tremblings!'' repeated Mr. Smith, shaking his head; ''but in the first place, is it certain that there have been tremblings? At the moment when the flames showed most sharply, I was on my farm of Wildon, less than a mile from the Great Eyrie. There was certainly a tumult in the air, but I felt no quivering of the earth.''

''But in the reports sent to Mr. Ward—''

''Reports made under the impulse of the panic,'' interrupted the mayor of Morganton. ''I said nothing of any earth tremors in mine.''

''But as to the flames which rose clearly above the crest?''

''Yes, as to those, Mr. Strock, that is different. I saw them; saw them with my own eyes, and the clouds certainly reflected them for miles around. Moreover noises certainly came from the crater of the Great Eyrie, hissings, as if a great boiler were letting off steam.''

''You have reliable testimony of this?''

''Yes, the evidence of my own ears.''

"And in the midst of this noise, Mr. Smith, did you believe that you heard that most remarkable of all the phenomena, a sound like the flapping of great wings?"

"I thought so, Mr. Strock; but what mighty bird could this be, which sped away after the flames had died down, and what wings could ever make such tremendous sounds. I therefore seriously question if this must not have been a deception of my imagination. The Great Eyrie a refuge for unknown monsters of the sky! Would they not have been seen long since, soaring above their immense nest of stone? In short, there is in all this a mystery which has not yet been solved."

"But we will solve it, Mr. Smith, if you will give me your aid."

"Surely, Mr. Strock; tomorrow we will start our campaign."

"Tomorrow." And on that word the mayor and I separated. I went to a hotel, and established myself for a stay which might be indefinitely prolonged. Then having dined, and written to Mr. Ward, I saw Mr. Smith again in the afternoon, and arranged to leave Morganton with him at daybreak.

Our first purpose was to undertake the ascent of the mountains, with the aid of two experienced guides. These men had ascended Mt. Mitchell and others of the highest peaks of the Blue Ridge. They had never, however, attempted the Great Eyrie, knowing that its walls of inaccessible cliffs defended it on every side. Moreover, before the recent startling occurrences the Great Eyrie had not particularly attracted the attention of tourists.

Mr. Smith knew the two guides personally as men daring, skillful and trustworthy. They would stop at no obstacle; and we were resolved to follow them through everything.

Moreover Mr. Smith remarked at the last that perhaps it was no longer as difficult as formerly to penetrate within the Great Eyrie.

"And why?" asked I.

"Because a huge block has recently broken away from the mountain side and perhaps it has left a practicable path or entrance."

"That would be a fortunate chance, Mr. Smith."

"We shall know all about it, Mr. Strock, no later than tomorrow."

"Till tomorrow, then."

Chapter 3

The Great Eyrie

The next day at dawn, Elias Smith and I left Morganton by a road, which winding along the left bank of the Catawba River, led to the village of Pleasant Garden. The guides accompanied us, Harry Horn, a man of thirty, and James Bruck, aged twenty-five. They were both natives of the region, and in constant demand among the tourists who climbed the peaks of the Blue Ridge and Cumberland Mountains.

A light wagon with two good horses was provided to carry us to the foot of the range. It contained provisions for two or three days, beyond which our trip surely would not be protracted. Mr. Smith had shown himself a generous provider both in meats and liquors. As to water, the mountain springs would furnish it in abundance, increased by the heavy rains, frequent in that region during springtime.

It is needless to add that the Mayor of Morganton in his role of hunter, had brought along his gun and his dog Nisko, who gamboled joyously about the wagon. Nisko, however, was to remain behind at the farm at Wildon, when we attempted our ascent. He could not possibly follow us up the Great Eyrie with its cliffs to scale and its crevasses to cross.

The day was beautiful, the fresh air in that climate is still cool of an April morning. A few fleecy clouds sped rapidly overhead, driven by a light breeze which swept across the long plains, from the distant Atlantic. The sun, peeping forth at intervals, illuminated all the fresh young verdure of the countryside.

An entire world animated the woods through which we passed. From before our equipage fled squirrels, field-mice, parakeets of brilliant colors and deafening loquacity. Opossums passed in hurried leaps, bearing their young in their pouches. Myriads of birds were scattered amid the foliage of banyans, palms, and masses of rhododendrons, so luxuriant that their thickets were impenetrable.

We arrived that evening at Pleasant Garden, where we were comfortably located for the night with the mayor of the town, a particular friend of Mr. Smith. Pleasant Garden proved little more than a village; but its mayor gave us a warm and generous reception, and we supped pleasantly in his charming home, which stood beneath the shades of some giant beech trees.

Naturally the conversation turned upon our attempt to explore the interior of the Great

Eyrie. "You are right," said our host. "Until we all know what is hidden within there, our people will remain uneasy."

"Has nothing new occurred," I asked, "since the last appearance of flames above the Great Eyrie?"

"Nothing, Mr. Strock. From Pleasant Garden we can see the entire crest of the mountain. Not a suspicious noise has come down to us. Not a spark has risen. If a legion of devils is in hiding there, they must have finished their infernal cookery, and soared away to some other haunt."

"Devils!" cried Mr. Smith. "Well, I hope they have not decamped without leaving some traces of their occupation, some parings of hoofs or horns or tails. We shall find them out."

On the morrow, the twenty-ninth of April, we started again at dawn. By the end of this second day, we expected to reach the farm of Wildon at the foot of the mountain. The country was much the same as before, except that our road led more steeply upward. Woods and marshes alternated, though the latter grew sparser, being drained by the sun as we approached the higher levels. The country was also less populous. There were only a few little hamlets, almost lost beneath the beech trees, a few lonely farms, abundantly watered by the many streams that rushed downward toward the Catawba River.

The smaller birds and beasts grew yet more numerous. "I am much tempted to take my gun," said Mr. Smith, "and to go off with

Nisko. This will be the first time that I have passed here without trying my luck with the partridges and hares. The good beasts will not recognize me. But not only have we plenty of provisions, but we have a bigger chase on hand today. The chase of a mystery."

"And let us hope," added I, "we do not come back disappointed hunters."

In the afternoon the whole chain of the Blue Ridge stretched before us at a distance of only six miles. The mountain crests were sharply outlined against the clear sky. Well wooded at the base, they grew more bare and showed only stunted evergreens toward the summit. There the scraggly trees, grotesquely twisted, gave to the rocky heights a bleak and bizarre appearance. Here and there the ridge rose in sharp peaks. On our right the Black Dome, nearly seven thousand feet high, reared its gigantic head, sparkling at times above the clouds.

"Have you ever climbed that dome, Mr. Smith?" I asked.

"No," answered he, "but I am told that it is a very difficult ascent. A few mountaineers have climbed it; but they report that it has no outlook commanding the crater of the Great Eyrie."

"That is so," said the guide, Harry Horn. "I have tried it myself."

"Perhaps," suggested I, "the weather was unfavorable."

"On the contrary, Mr. Strock, it was unusually clear. But the wall of the Great Eyrie on that side rose so high, it completely hid the interior."

"Forward," cried Mr. Smith. "I shall not be sorry to set foot where no person has ever stepped, or even looked, before."

Certainly on this day the Great Eyrie looked tranquil enough. As we gazed upon it, there rose from its heights neither smoke nor flame.

Toward five o'clock our expedition halted at the Wildon farm, where the tenants warmly welcomed their landlord. The farmer assured us that nothing notable had happened about the Great Eyrie for some time. We supped at a common table with all the people of the farm; and our sleep that night was sound and wholly untroubled by premonitions of the future.

On the morrow, before break of day, we set out for the ascent of the mountain. The height of the Great Eyrie scarce exceeds five thousand feet. A modest altitude, often surpassed in this section of the Alleghenies. As we were already more than three thousand feet above sea level, the fatigue of the ascent could not be great. A few hours should suffice to bring us to the crest of the crater. Of course, difficulties might present themselves, precipices to scale, clefts and breaks in the ridge might necessitate painful and even dangerous detours. This was the unknown, the spur to our attempt. As I said, our guides knew no more than we upon this point. What made me anxious, was, of course, the common report that the Great Eyrie was wholly inaccessible. But this remained unproven. And then there was the new chance that a fallen block had left a breach in the rocky wall.

"At last," said Mr. Smith to me, after lighting the first pipe of the twenty or more which he smoked each day, "we are well started. As to whether the ascent will take more or less time—"

"In any case, Mr. Smith," interrupted I, "you and I are fully resolved to pursue our quest to the end."

"Fully resolved, Mr. Strock."

"My chief has charged me to snatch the secret from this demon of the Great Eyrie."

"We will snatch it from him, willing or unwilling," vowed Mr. Smith, calling Heaven to witness. "Even if we have to search the very bowels of the mountain."

"As it may happen, then," said I, "that our excursion will be prolonged beyond today, it will be well to look to our provisions."

"Be easy, Mr. Strock; our guides have food for two days in their knapsacks, besides what we carry ourselves. Moreover, though I left my brave Nisko at the farm, I have my gun. Game will be plentiful in the woods and gorges of the lower part of the mountain, and perhaps at the top we shall find a fire to cook it, already lighted."

"Already lighted, Mr. Smith?"

"And why not, Mr. Stock? These flames! These superb flames, which have so terrified our country folk! Is their fire absolutely cold, is no spark to be found beneath their ashes? And then, if this is truly a crater, is the volcano so wholly extinct that we cannot find there a single ember? Bah! This would be but a poor volcano if it hasn't enough fire even to cook an egg or roast a potato. Come, I rep**eat, we** shall see! We shall see!''

At that point of the investigation I had, I confess, no opinion formed. I had my orders to examine the Great Eyrie. If it proved harmless, I would announce it, and people would be reassured. But at heart, I must admit, I had the very natural desire of a man possessed by the demon of curiosity. I should be glad, both for my own sake, and for the renown which would attach to my mission if the Great Eyrie proved the center of the most remarkable phenomena— of which I would discover the cause.

Our ascent began in this order. The two guides went in front to seek out the most practical paths. Elias Smith and I followed more leisurely. We mounted by a narrow and not very steep gorge amid rocks and trees. A tiny stream trickled downward under our feet. During the rainy season or after a heavy shower, the water doubtless bounded from rock to rock in tumultuous cascades. But it evidently was fed only by the rain, for now we could scarcely trace its course. It could not be the outlet of any lake within the Great Eyrie.

After an hour of climbing, the slope became so steep that we had to turn, now to the right, now to the left; and our progress was much delayed. Soon the gorge became wholly impracticable; its clifflike sides offered no sufficient foothold. We had to cling by branches, to crawl upon our knees. At this rate the top would not be reached before sundown.

"Faith!" cried Mr. Smith, stopping for breath, "I realize why the climbers of the Great Eyrie have been few, so few, that it has never been ascended within my knowledge."

"The fact is," I responded, "that it would be much toil for very little profit. And if we had not special reasons to persist in our attempt—"

"You never said a truer word," declared Harry Horn. "My comrades and I have scaled the Black Dome several times, but we never met such obstacles as these."

"The difficulties seem almost impassable," added James Bruck.

The question now was to determine to which side we should turn for a new route; to right, as to left, arose impenetrable masses of trees and bushes. In truth even the scaling of cliffs would have been more easy. Perhaps if we could get above this wooded slope we could advance with surer foot. Now, we could only go ahead blindly, and trust to the instincts of our two guides. James Bruck was especially useful. I believe that the gallant lad would have equalled a monkey in lightness and a wild goat in agility. Unfortunately, neither Elias Smith nor I was able to climb where he could.

However, when it is a matter of real need with me, I trust I shall never be backward, being resolute by nature and well-trained in bodily exercise. Where James Bruck went, I was determined to go, also; though it might cost me some uncomfortable falls. But it was not the same with the first magistrate of Morganton, less young, less vigorous, larger, stouter, and less persistent than we others. Plainly he made every effort, not to retard our progress, but he panted like a seal, and soon I insisted on his stopping to rest.

In short, it was evident that the ascent of the Gret Eyrie would require far more time than we had estimated. We had expected to reach the foot of the rocky wall before eleven o'clock, but we now saw that mid-day would still find us several hundred feet below it.

Toward ten o'clock, after repeated attempts to discover some more practical route, after numberless turnings and returnings, one of the guides gave the signal to halt. We found ourselves at last on the upper border of the heavy wood. The trees, more thinly spaced, permitted us a glimpse upward to the base of the rocky wall which constituted the true Great Eyrie.

"Whew!" exclaimed Mr. Smith, leaning against a mighty pine tree. "A little repose, and even a little repast would not go badly."

"We will rest an hour," said I.

"Yes; after working our lungs and our legs, we will make our stomachs work."

We were all agreed on this point. A rest would certainly freshen us. Our only cause for inquietude was now the appearance of the precipitous slope above us. We looked up toward one of those bare strips called in that region, slides. Amid this loose earth, these yielding stones, and these abrupt rocks there was no roadway.

Harry Horn said to his comrade, "It will not be easy."

"Perhaps impossible," responded Bruck.

Their comments caused me secret uneasiness. If I returned without even having scaled the mountain, my mission would be a complete failure, without speaking of the torture to my curiosity. And when I stood again before Mr. Ward, shamed and confused, I should cut but a sorry figure.

We opened our knapsacks and lunched moderately on bread and cold meat. Our repast finished, in less than half an hour, Mr. Smith sprang up eager to push forward once more. James Bruck took the lead; and we had only to follow him as best we could.

We advanced slowly. Our guides did not attempt to conceal their doubt and hesitation. Soon Horn left us and went far ahead to spy out which road promised most chance of success.

Twenty minutes later he returned and led us onward toward the northwest. It was on this side that the Black Dome rose at a distance of three or four miles. Our path was still difficult and painful, amid the sliding stones, held in place only occasionally by wiry bushes. At length after a weary struggle, we gained some two hundred feet further upward and found ourselves facing a great gash, which broke the earth at this spot. Here and there were scattered roots recently uptorn, branches broken off, huge stones reduced to powder, as if an avalanche had rushed down this flank of the mountain.

"That must be the path taken by the huge block which broke away from the Great Eyrie," commented James Bruck.

"No doubt," answered Mr. Smith, "and I think we had better follow the road that it has made for us."

It was indeed this gash that Harry Horn had selected for our ascent. Our feet found lodgment in the firmer earth which had resisted the passage of the monster rock. Our task thus became much easier, and our progress was in a straight line upward, so that toward half past eleven we reached the upper border of the "slide."

Before us, less than a hundred feet away, but towering a hundred feet straight upwards in the air rose the rocky wall which formed the final crest, the last defense of the Great Eyrie.

From this side, the summit of the wall showed capriciously irregular, rising in rude towers and jagged needles. At one point the outline appeared to be an enormous eagle silhouetted against the sky, just ready to take flight. Upon this side, at least, the precipice was insurmountable.

"Rest a minute," said Mr. Smith, "and we will see if it is possible to make our way around the base of this cliff."

"At any rate," said Harry Horn, "the great block must have fallen from this part of the cliff; and it has left no breach for entering."

They were both right; we must seek entrance elsewhere. After a rest of ten minutes, we clambered up close to the foot of the wall, and began to make a circuit of its base.

Assuredly the Great Eyrie now took on to my eyes an aspect absolutely fantastic. Its heights seemed peopled by dragons and huge monsters. If chimeras, griffins, and all the creations of mythology had appeared to guard it, I should have been scarcely surprised.

With great difficulty and not without danger we continued our tour of this circumvallation, where it seemed that nature had worked as man does, with careful regularity. Nowhere was there any break in the fortification; nowhere a fault in the strata by which one might clamber up. Always this mighty wall, a hundred feet in height!

After an hour and a half of this laborious circuit, we regained our starting place. I could not conceal my disappointment, and Mr. Smith was not less chagrined than I.

"A thousand devils!" cried he. "We know no better than before what is inside this confounded Great Eyrie, nor even if it is a crater."

"Volcano, or not," said I, "there are no suspicious noises now; neither smoke nor flame rises above it; nothing whatever threatens an eruption."

This was true. A profound silence reigned around us; and a perfectly clear sky shone overhead. We tasted the perfect calm of great altitudes.

It was worth noting that the circumference of the huge wall was about twelve or fifteen hundred feet. As to the space enclosed within, we could scarce reckon that without knowing the thickness of the encompassing wall. The surroundings were absolutely deserted.

Probably not a living creature ever mounted to this height, except the few birds of prey which soared high above us.

Our watches showed three o'clock, and Mr. Smith cried in disgust, "What is the use of stopping here all day! We shall learn nothing more. We must make a start, Mr. Strock, if we want to get back to Pleasant Garden tonight."

I made no answer, and did not move from where I was seated; so he called again, "Come on, Mr. Strock; you don't answer."

In truth, it cut me deeply to abandon our effort, to descend the slope without having achieved my mission. I felt an imperious need of persisting; my curiosity had redoubled. But what could I do? Could I tear open this unyielding earth? Overleap the mighty cliff? Throwing one last defiant glare at the Great Eyrie, I followed my companions.

The return was effected without great difficulty. We had only to slide down where we had so laboriously scrambled up. Before five o'clock we descended the last slopes of the mountain, and the farmer of Wildon welcomed us to a much needed meal.

"Then you didn't get inside?" said he.

"No," responded Mr. Smith, "and I believe that the inside exists only in the imagination of our country folk."

At half past eight our carriage drew up before the house of the Mayor of Pleasant Garden, where we passed the night. While I strove vainly to sleep, I asked myself if I should not stop there in the village and organize a new ascent. But what better chance had it of succeeding than the first? The wisest course was, doubtless, to return to Washington and consult Mr. Ward.

So, the next day, having rewarded our two guides, I took leave of Mr. Smith at Morganton, and that same evening left by train for Washington.

Chapter 4

A Meeting of the Automobile Club

Was the mystery of the Great Eyrie to be solved some day by chances beyond our imagining? That was known only to the future. And was the solution a matter of the first importance? That was beyond doubt, since the safety of the people of western Carolina perhaps depended upon it.

Yet a fortnight after my return to Washington, public attention was wholly distracted from this problem by another very different in nature, but equally astonishing.

Toward the middle of that month of May the newspapers of Pennsylvania informed their readers of some strange occurrences in different parts of the state. On the roads which radiated from Philadelphia, the chief city, there circulated an extraordinary vehicle, of which no one could describe the form, or the nature, or even the size, so rapidly did it rush past. It was an automobile; all were agreed on that. But as to what motor drove it, only imagination could say; and when the popular imagination is aroused, what limit is there to its hypotheses?

At that period the most improved automobiles, whether driven by steam, gasoline, or electricity, could not accomplish much more than sixty miles an hour, a speed that the railroads, with their most rapid expresses, scarce exceed on the best lines of America and Europe. Now, this new automobile which was astonishing the world, traveled at more than double this speed.

It is needless to add that such a rate constituted an extreme danger on the highroads, as much so for vehicles, as for pedestrians. This rushing mass, coming like a thunderbolt, preceded by a formidable rumbling, caused a whirlwind, which tore the branches from the trees along the road, terrified the animals browsing in adjoining fields, and scattered and killed the birds, which could not resist the suction of the tremendous air currents engendered by its passage.

And, a bizarre detail, to which the newspapers drew particular attention, the surface of the roads was scarcely even scratched by the wheels of the apparition, which left behind it no such ruts as are usually made by heavy vehicles. At most there was a light touch, a mere brushing of the dust.

It was only the tremendous speed which raised behind the vehicle such whirlwinds of dust.

"It is probable," commented the New York *Herald*, "that the extreme rapidity of motion destroys the weight."

Naturally there were protests from all sides. It was impossible to permit the mad speed of this apparition which threatened to overthrow and destroy everything in its passage, equipages and people. But how could it be stopped? No one knew to whom the vehicle belonged, nor whence it came, nor whither it went. It was seen but for an instant as it darted forward like a bullet in its dizzy flight. How could one seize a cannonball in the air, as it leaped from the mouth of the gun?

I repeat, there was no evidence as to the character of the propelling engine. It left behind it no smoke, no steam, no odor of gasoline, or any other oil. It seemed probable therefore, that the vehicle ran by electricity, and that its accumulators were of an unknown model, using some unknown fluid.

The public imagination, highly excited, readily accepted every sort of rumor about this mysterious automobile. It was said to be a supernatural car. It was driven by a specter, by one of the chauffeurs of hell, a goblin from another world, a monster escaped from some mythological menagerie, in short, the devil in person, who could defy all human intervention, having at his command invisible and infinite satanic powers.

But even Satan himself had no right to run at

such speed over the roads of the United States without a special permit, without a number on his car, and without a regular license. And it was certain that not a single municipality had given him permission to go two hundred miles an hour. Public security demanded that some means be found to unmask the secret of this terrible chauffeur.

Moreover, it was not only Pennsylvania that served as the theater of his sportive eccentricities. The police reported his appearance in other states; in Kentucky near Frankfort; in Ohio near Columbus; in Tennessee near Nashville; in Missouri near Jefferson; and finally in Illinois in the neighborhood of Chicago.

The alarm having been given, it became the duty of the authorities to take steps against this public danger. To arrest or even to halt an apparition moving at such speed was scarcely practicable. A better way would be to erect across the roads solid gateways with which the flying machine must come in contact sooner or later, and be smashed into a thousand pieces.

"Nonsense!" declared the incredulous. "This madman would know well how to circle around such obstructions."

"And if necessary," added others, "the machine would leap over the barriers."

"And if he is indeed the devil, he has, as a former angel, presumably preserved his wings, and so he will take to flight."

But this last was but the suggestion of foolish old gossips who did not stop to study the matter.

For if the King of Hades possessed a pair of wings, why did he obstinately persist in running around on the earth at the risk of crushing his own subjects, when he might more easily have hurled himself through space as free as a bird.

Such was the situation when, in the last week of May, a fresh event occurred, which seemed to show that the United States was indeed helpless in the hands of some unapproachable monster. And after the New World, would not the Old in its turn, be desecrated by the mad career of this remarkable automobilist?

The following occurrence was reported in all the newspapers of the Union, and with what comments and outcries it is easy to imagine.

A race was to be held by the Automobile Club of Wisconsin, over the roads of that state of which Madison is the capital. The route laid out formed an excellent track, about two hundred miles in length, starting from Prairie du Chien on the western frontier, passing by Madison and ending a little above Milwaukee on the borders of Lake Michigan. Except for the Japanese road between Nikko and Namode, bordered by giant cypresses, there is no better track in the world than this of Wisconsin. It runs straight and level as an arrow for sometimes fifty miles at a stretch. Many and noted were the machines entered for this great race. Every kind of motor vehicle was permitted to compete, even motorcycles, as well as automobiles. The machines were of all makes and nationalities. The sum of the different prizes reached fifty thousand dollars, so that the race was sure to be desperately contested. New records were expected to be made.

Calculating on the maximum speed hitherto attained, of perhaps eighty miles an hour, this international contest covering two hundred miles would last about three hours. And, to avoid all danger, the state authorities of Wisconsin had forbidden all other traffic between Prairie du Chien and Milwaukee during three hours on the morning of the thirtieth of May. Thus, if there were any accidents, those who suffered would be themselves to blame.

There was an enormous crowd; and it was not composed only of the people of Wisconsin. Many thousands gathered from the neighboring states of Illinois, Michigan, Iowa, and even from New York. Among the sportsmen assembled were many foreigners, English, French, Germans and Austrians, each nationality, of course, supporting the chauffeurs of its land. Moreover, as this was the United States, the country of the greatest gamblers of the world, bets were made of every sort and of enormous amounts.

The start was to be made at eight o'clock in the morning; and to avoid crowding and the accidents which must result from it, the automobiles were to follow each other at two minute intervals, along the road whose borders were black with spectators.

The first ten racers, numbered by lot, were dispatched between eight o'clock and twenty minutes past. Unless there was some disastrous accident, some of these machines would surely arrive at the goal by eleven o'clock. The others followed in order.

An hour and a half had passed. There remained but a single contestant at Prairie du Chien. Word was sent back and forth by telephone every five minutes as to the order of the racers. Midway between Madison and Milwaukee, the lead was held by a machine of Renault brothers, four-cylindered, of twenty horsepower, and with Michelin tires. It was closely followed by a Harvard-Watson car and by a Dion-Bouton. Some accidents had already occurred, other machines were hopelessly behind. Not more than a dozen would contest the finish. Several chauffeurs had been injured, but not seriously. And even had they been killed, the death of men is but a detail, not considered of great importance in that astonishing country of America.

Naturally the excitement became more intense as one approached the finishing line near Milwaukee. There were assembled the most curious, the most interested; and there the passions of the moment were unchained. By ten o'clock it was evident, that the first prize, twenty thousand dollars, lay between five machines, two American, two French, and one English. Imagine, therefore, the fury with which bets were being made under the influence of national pride. The regular book makers could scarcely meet the demands of those who wished to wager. Offers and amounts were hurled from lip to lip with feverish rapidity. "One to three on the Harvard-Watson!"

"One to two on the Dion-Bouton!"

"Even money on the Renault!"

These cries rang along the line of spectators at each new announcement from the telephones.

Suddenly at half-past nine by the town clock of Prairie du Chien, two miles beyond the town was heard a tremendous noise and rumbling which proceeded from the midst of a flying cloud of dust accompanied by shrieks like those of a naval siren.

Scarcely had the crowds time to draw to one side, to escape a destruction which would have included hundreds of victims. The cloud swept by like a hurricane. No one could distinguish what it was that passed with such speed. There was no exaggeration in saying that its rate was at least one hundred and fifty miles an hour.

The apparition passed and disappeared in an instant, leaving behind it a long train of white dust, as an express locomotive leaves behind a train of smoke. Evidently it was an automobile with a most extraordinary motor. If it maintained this arrowlike speed, it would reach the contestants in the forefront of the race; it would pass them with this speed double their own; it would arrive first at the goal.

And then from all parts arose an uproar, as soon as the spectators had nothing more to fear.

"It is that infernal machine."

"Yes; the one the police cannot stop."

"But it has not been heard of for a fortnight."

"It was supposed to be done for, destroyed, gone forever."

"It is a devil's car, driven by hellfire, and with Satan driving!"

In truth, if he were not the devil, who could this mysterious chauffeur be, driving with this unbelievable velocity, his no less mysterious machine? At least it was beyond doubt that this was the same machine which had already attracted so much attention. If the police believed that they had frightened it away, there it was never to be heard of more, well the police were mistaken—which happens in America as elsewhere.

The first stunned moment of surprise having passed, many people rushed to the telephones to warn those further along the route of the danger which menaced, not only the people, but the automobiles scattered along the road.

When this terrible madman arrived like an avalanche they would be smashed to pieces, ground into powder, annihilated!

And from the collision might not the destroyer himself emerge safe and sound? He must be so adroit, this chauffeur of chauffeurs, he must handle his machine with such perfection of eye and hand, that he knew, no doubt, how to escape from every situation. Fortunately the Wisconsin authorities had taken such precautions that the road would be clear except for contesting automobiles. But what right had this machine among them!

And what said the racers themselves, who, warned by telephone, had to sheer aside from the road in their struggle for the grand prize? By their estimate, this amazing vehicle was going at least one hundred and thirty miles an hour. Fast as was their speed, it shot by them at such a rate that they could hardly make out even the shape of the machine, a sort of lengthened spindle, probably not over thirty feet long. Its wheels spun with such velocity that they could scarce be seen. For the rest, the machine left behind it neither smoke nor scent.

As for the driver, hidden in the interior of his machine, he had been quite invisible. He remained as unknown as when he had first appeared on the various roads throughout the country.

Milwaukee was promptly warned of the coming of this interloper. Fancy the excitement the news caused! The immediate purpose agreed upon was to stop this projectile, to erect across its route an obstacle against which it would smash into a thousand pieces. But was there time? Would not the machine appear at any moment? And what need was there, since the track ended on the edge of Lake Michigan, and so the vehicle would be forced to stop there anyway, unless its supernatural driver could ride the water as well as the land.

Here, also, as all along the route, the most extravagant suggestions were offered. Even those who would not admit that the mysterious chauffeur must be Satan in person, allowed that he might be some monster escaped from the fantastic visions of the apocalypse.

And now there were no longer minutes to wait. Any second might bring the expected apparition.

It was not yet eleven o'clock when a rumbling was heard far down the track, and the dust rose in violent whirlwinds. Harsh whistlings shrieked through the air warning all to give passage to the monster.

It did not slacken speed at the finish. Lake Michigan was not half a mile beyond, and the machine must certainly be hurled into the water!

Could it be that the mechanician was no longer master of his mechanism?

There could be little doubt of it. Like a shooting star, the vehicle flashed through Milwaukee. When it had passed the city, would it plunge itself to destruction in the waters of Lake Michigan?

At any rate when it disappeared at a slight bend in the road no trace was to be found of its passage.

Chapter 5
Along the Shores of New England

At the time when the newspapers were filled with these reports, I was again in Washington. On my return I had presented myself at my chief's office, but had been unable to see him. Family affairs had suddenly called him away, to be absent some weeks. Mr. Ward, however, undoubtedly knew of the failure of my mission. The newspapers, especially those of North Carolina, had given full details of our ascent of the Great Eyrie.

Naturally, I was much annoyed by this delay which further fretted my restless curiosity. I could turn to no other plans for the future. Could I give up the hope of learning the secret of the Great

Eyrie? No! I would return to the attack a dozen times if necessary, and despite every failure.

Surely, the winning of access within those walls was not a task beyond human power. A scaffolding might be raised to the summit of the cliff; or a tunnel might be pierced through its depth. Our engineers met problems more difficult every day. But in this case it was necessary to consider the expense which might easily grow out of proportion to the advantages to be gained. A tunnel would cost many thousand dollars, and what good would it accomplish beyond satisfying the public curiosity and my own?

My personal resources were wholly insufficient for the achievement. Mr. Ward, who held the government's funds, was away. I even thought of trying to interest some millionaire. Oh, if I could but have promised one of them some gold or silver mines within the mountain! But such an hypothesis was not admissable. The chain of the Appalachians is not situated in a gold bearing region like that of the Pacific mountains, the Transvaal, or Australia.

It was not until the fifteenth of June that Mr. Ward returned to duty. Despite my lack of success he received me warmly. "Here is our poor Strock!" cried he, at my entrance. "Our poor Strock, who has failed!"

"No more, Mr. Ward, than if you had charged me to investigate the surface of the moon," answered I. "We found ourselves face to face with purely natural obstacles insurmountable with the forces then at our command."

"I do not doubt that, Strock, I do not doubt that in the least. Nevertheless, the fact remains that you have discovered nothing of what is going on within the Great Eyrie."

"Nothing, Mr. Ward."

"You saw no sign of fire?"

"None."

"And you heard no suspicious noises whatever?"

"None."

"Then it is still uncertain if there is really a volcano there?"

"Still uncertain, Mr. Ward. But if it is there, we have good reason to believe that it has sunk into a profound sleep."

"Still," returned Mr. Ward, "there is nothing to show that it will not wake up again any day, Strock. It is not enough that a volcano should sleep, it must be absolutely extinguished—unless indeed all these threatening rumors have been born solely in the Carolinian imagination."

"That is not possible, sir," I said. "Both Mr. Smith, the mayor of Morganton and his friend the mayor of Pleasant Garden, are reliable men. And they speak from their own knowledge in this matter. Flames have certainly risen above the Great Eyrie. Strange noises have issued from it. There can be no doubt whatever of the reality of these phenomena."

"Granted," declared Mr. Ward. "I admit that the evidence is unassailable. So the deduction to be drawn is that the Great Eyrie has not yet given up its secret."

"If we are determined to know it, Mr. Ward, the solution is only a solution of expense. Pickaxes and dynamite would soon conquer those walls."

"No doubt," responded the chief. "But such an undertaking hardly seems justified, since the mountain is now quiet. We will wait awhile and perhaps nature herself will disclose her mystery."

"Mr. Ward, believe me that I regret deeply that I have been unable to solve the problem you entrusted to me," I said.

"Nonsense! Do not upset yourself, Strock. Take your defeat philosophically. We cannot always be successful, even in the police. How many criminals escape us! I believe we should never capture one of them, if they were a little more intelligent and less imprudent, and if they did not compromise themselves so stupidly. Nothing, it seems to me, would be easier than to plan a crime, a theft or an assassination, and to execute it without arousing any suspicions, or leaving any traces to be followed. You understand, Strock, I do not want to give our criminals lessons; I much prefer to have them remain as they are. Nevertheless there are many whom the police will never be able to track down."

On this matter I shared absolutely the opinion of my chief. It is among rascals that one finds the most fools. For this very reason I had been much surprised that none of the authorities had been able to throw any light upon the recent performances of the "demon automobile." And when Mr. Ward brought up this subject, I did not conceal from him my astonishment.

He pointed out that the vehicle was practically unpursuable; that in its earlier appearances, it had apparently vanished from all roads even before a telephone message could be sent ahead! Active and numerous police agents had been spread throughout the country, but not one of them had encountered the delinquent. He did not move continuously from place to place, even at his amazing speed, but seemed to appear only for a moment and then to vanish into thin air. True, he had at length remained visible along the entire route from Prairie du Chien to Milwaukee, and he had covered in less than an hour and a half this track of two hundred miles.

But since then, there had been no news whatever of the machine. Arrived at the end of the route, driven onward by its own impetus, unable to stop, had it indeed been engulfed within the waters of Lake Michigan? Must we conclude that the machine and its driver had both perished, that there was no longer any danger to be feared from either? The great majority of the public refused to accept this conclusion. They fully expected the machine to reappear.

Mr. Ward frankly admitted that the whole matter seemed to him most extraordinary; and I shared his view. Assuredly if this infernal chauffeur did not return, his apparition would have to be placed among those superhuman mysteries which it is not given to man to understand.

We had fully discussed this affair, the chief and I; and I thought that our interview was at an end, when, after pacing the room for a few moments, he said abruptly, "Yes, what happened there at Milwaukee was very strange. But here is something no less so!"

With this he handed me a report which he had received from Boston, on a subject of which the evening papers had just begun to apprise their readers. While I read it, Mr. Ward was summoned from the room. I seated myself by the window and studied with extreme attention the matter of the report.

For some days the waters along the coast of Maine, Connecticut, and Massachusetts had been the scene of an appearance which no one could exactly describe. A moving body would appear amid the waters, some two or three miles off shore, and go through rapid evolutions. It would flash for a while back and forth among the waves and then dart out of sight.

The body moved with such lightning speed that the best telescopes could hardly follow it. Its length did not seem to exceed thirty feet. Its cigar-shaped form and greenish color, made it difficult to distinguish against the background of the ocean. It had been most frequently observed along the coast between Cape Cod and Nova Scotia. From Providence, from Boston, from Portsmouth, and from Portland motor boats and steam launches had repeatedly attempted to approach this moving body and even to give it chase. They could not get anywhere near it. Pursuit seemed useless. It darted like an arrow beyond the range of view.

Naturally, widely differing opinions were held as to the nature of this object. But no hypothesis rested on any secure basis. Seamen were as much at a loss as others. At first sailors thought it must be some great fish, like a whale. But it is well known that all these animals come to the surface with a certain regularity to breathe, and spout up columns of mingled air and water. Now, this strange animal, if it was an animal, had never "blown" as the whalers say; nor, had it ever made any noises of breathing. Yet if it were not one of these huge marine mammals, how was the unknown monster to be classed? Did it belong among the legendary dwellers in the deep, the krakens, the octopuses, the leviathans, the famous sea serpents?

At any rate, since this monster, whatever it was, had appeared along the New England shores, the little fishing-smacks and pleasure boats dared not venture forth. Wherever it appeared the boats fled to the nearest harbor, as was but prudent. If the animal was of a ferocious character, none cared to await its attack.

As to the large ships and coast steamers, they had nothing to fear from any monster, whale or otherwise. Several of them had seen this creature at a distance of some miles. But when they attempted to approach, it fled rapidly away. One day, even, a fast United States gunboat went out from Boston, if not to pursue the monster, at least to send after it a few cannon shot. Almost instantly the animal disappeared, and the attempt was vain. As yet, however, the monster had shown no intention of attacking either boats or people.

At this moment Mr. Ward returned and I

interrupted my reading to say, "There seems as yet no reason to complain of this sea serpent. It flees before big ships. It does not pursue little ones. Feeling and intelligence are not very strong in fishes."

"Yet their emotions exist, Strock, and if strongly aroused—"

"But Mr. Ward, the beast seems not at all dangerous. One of two things will happen. Either it will presently quit these coasts, or finally it will be captured and we shall be able to study it at our leisure here in the museum of Washington."

"And if it is not a marine animal?" asked Mr. Ward.

"What else can it be?" I protested in surprise.

"Finish your reading," said Mr. Ward.

I did so; and found that in the second part of the report, my chief had underlined some passages in red pencil.

For some time no one had doubted that this was an animal; and that, if it were vigorously pursued, it would at last be driven from our shores. But a change of opinion had come about. People began to ask if, instead of a fish, this were not some new and remarkable kind of boat.

Certainly in that case its engine must be one of amazing power. Perhaps the inventor before selling the secret of his invention, sought to attract public attention and to astound the maritime world. Such surety in the movements of his boat, grace in its every evolution, such ease in defying pursuit by its arrow-like speed, surely, these were enough to arouse world-wide curiosity!

At that time great progress had been made in the manufacture of marine engines. Huge transatlantic steamers completed the ocean passage in five days. And the engineers had not yet spoken their last word. Neither were the navies of the world behind-hand. The cruisers, the torpedo boats, the torpedo-destroyers, could match the swiftest steamers of the Atlantic and Pacific, or of the Indian trade.

If, however, this were a boat of some new design, there had as yet been no opportunity to observe its form. As to the engines which drove it, they must be of a power far beyond the fastest known. By what force they worked, was equally a problem. Since the boat had no sails, it was not driven by the wind; and since it had no smoke stack, it was not driven by steam.

At this point in the report, I again paused in my reading and considered the comment I wished to make.

"What are you puzzling over, Strock?" demanded my chief.

"It is this, Mr. Ward; the motive power of this so-called boat must be as tremendous and as unknown as that of the remarkable automobile which has so amazed us all."

"So that is your idea, is it, Strock?"

"Yes, Mr. Ward."

There was but one conclusion to be drawn. If the mysterious chauffeur had disappeared, if he had perished with his machine in Lake Michigan, it was equally important now to win the secret of this no less mysterious navigator. And it must be won before he in his turn plunged into the abyss of the ocean. Was it not the interest of the inventor to disclose his invention? Would not the American government or any other give him any price he chose to ask?

Yet unfortunately, since the inventor of the terrestrial apparition had persisted in preserving his incognito, was it not to be feared that the inventor of the marine apparition would equally preserve his? Even if the first machine still existed, it was no longer heard from; and would not the second, in the same way, after having disclosed its powers, disappear in its turn, without a single trace?

What gave weight to this probability was that since the arrival of this report at Washington twenty-four hours before, the presence of the extraordinary boat had not been announced from anywhere along the shore. Neither had it been seen on any other coast. Though, of course, the assertion that it would not reappear at all, would have been hazardous, to say the least.

I noted another interesting and possibly important point. It was a singular coincidence which indeed Mr. Ward suggested to me, at the same moment that I was considering it. This was that only after the disappearance of the wonderful automobile had the no less wonderful boat come in view. Moreover, their engines both possessed a most dangerous power of locomotion. If both should go rushing at the same time over the face of the world, the same danger would threaten mankind everywhere, in boats, in vehicles, and on foot. Therefore it was absolutely necessary that the police should in some mannner interfere to protect the public ways of travel.

This is what Mr. Ward pointed out to me; and our duty was obvious. But how could we accomplish this task? We discussed the matter for some time; and I was just about to leave when Mr. Ward made one last suggestion.

"Have you not observed, Strock," said he, "that there is a sort of fantastic resemblance between the general appearance of this boat and this automobile?"

"There is something of the sort, Mr. Ward."

"Well, is it not possible that the two are one?"

Chapter 6

The First Letter

After leaving Mr. Ward I returned to my home in Long Street. There I had plenty of time to consider this strange case uninterrupted by either wife or children. My household consisted solely of an ancient servant, who having been formerly in the service of my mother, had now continued for fifteen years in mine.

Two months before I had obtained a leave of absence. It had still two weeks to run, unless some unforeseen circumstance interrupted it, some mission which could not be delayed. This leave, as I have shown, had already been interrupted for four days by my exploration of the Great Eyrie.

And now was it not my duty to abandon my vacation, and endeavor to throw light upon the remarkable events of which the road to Milwaukee and the shore of New England had been in turn the scene? I would have given much to solve the twin mysteries, but how was it possible to follow the track of this automobile or this boat?

Seated in my easy chair after breakfast, with my pipe lighted, I opened my newspaper. To what should I turn? Politics interested me but little, with its eternal strife between the Republicans and the Democrats. Neither did I care for the news of society, nor for the sporting page. You will not be surprised, then, that my first idea was to see if there was any news from North Carolina about the Great Eyrie. There was little hope of this, however, for Mr. Smith had promised to telegraph me at once if anything occurred. I felt quite sure that the mayor of Morganton was as eager for information and as watchful as I could have been myself. The paper told me nothing new. It dropped idly from my hand, and I remained deep in thought.

What most frequently recurred to me was the suggestion of Mr. Ward that perhaps the automobile and the boat which had attracted our attention were in reality one and the same. Very probably, at least, the two machines had been built by the same hand. And beyond doubt, these were similar engines, which generated this remarkable speed, more than doubling the previous records of earth and sea.

"The same inventor!" repeated I.

Evidently this hypothesis had strong grounds. The fact that the two machines had not yet appeared at the same time added weight to the idea. I murmured to myself, "After the mystery of Great Eyrie, comes that of Milwaukee and Boston. Will this new problem be as difficult to solve as was the other?"

I noted idly that this new affair had a general resemblance to the other, since both menaced the security of the general public. To be sure, only the inhabitants of the Blue Ridge region had been in danger from an eruption or possible earthquake at Great Eyrie. While now, on every road of the United States, or along every league of its coasts and harbors, every inhabitant was in danger from this vehicle or this boat, with its sudden appearance and insane speed.

I found that, as was to be expected, the newspapers not only suggested, but enlarged upon the dangers of the case. Timid people everywhere were much alarmed. My old servant, naturally credulous and superstitious, was particularly upset. That same day after dinner, as she was clearing away the things, she stopped before me, a water bottle in one hand, the serviette in the other, and asked anxiously, "Is there no news, sir?"

"None," I answered knowing well to what she referred.

"The automobile has not come back?"

"No."

"Nor the boat?"

"Nor the boat. There is no news even in the best-informed papers."

"But—your secret police information?"

"We are no wiser."

"Then, sir, if you please, of what use are the police?"

It is a question which had phased me more than once.

"Now you see what will happen," continued the old housekeeper, complainingly. "Some fine morning, he will come without warning, this terrible chauffeur, and rush down our street here, and kill us all!"

"Good! When that happens there will be some chance of catching him."

"He will never be arrested, sir."

"Why not?"

"Because he is the devil himself, and you can't arrest the devil!"

Decidedly, thought I, the devil has many uses; and if he did not exist we would have to invent him, to give people some way of explaining the inexplicable. It was he who lit the flames of the Great Eyrie. It was he who smashed the record in the Wisconsin race. It is he who is scurrying along the shores of Connecticut and Massachussetts. But putting to one side this evil spirit who is so necessary, for the convenience of the ignorant, there was no doubt that we were facing a most bewildering problem. Had both of these machines disappeared forever? They had passed like a meteor, like a star shooting through space; and in a hundred years the adventure would become a legend, much to the taste of the gossips of the next century.

For several days the newspapers of America

and even those of Europe continued to discuss these events. Editorials crowded upon editorials. Rumors were added to rumors. Storytellers of every kind crowded to the front. The public of two continents was interested. In some parts of Europe there was even jealousy that America should have been chosen as the field of such an experience. If these marvelous inventors were American, then their country, their army and navy, would have a great advantage over others. The United States might acquire an incontestable superiority.

Under the date of the tenth of June, a New York paper published a carefully studied article on this phase of the subject. Comparing the speed of the swiftest known vessels with the smallest minimum of speed which could possibly be assigned to the new boat, the article demonstrated that if the United States secured this secret, Europe would be but three days away from her, while she would still be five days from Europe.

If our own police had searched diligently to discover the mystery of the Great Eyrie, the secret service of every country in the world was now interested in these new problems.

Mr. Ward referred to the matter each time I saw him. Our chat would begin by his rallying me about my ill-success in Carolina, and I would respond by reminding him that success there was only a question of expense.

"Never mind, my good Strock," said he, "there will come a chance for our clever inspector to regain his laurels. Take now this affair of the

57

automobile and the boat. If you could clear that up in advance of all the detectives of the world, what an honor it would be to our department! What glory for you!"

"It certainly would, Mr. Ward. And if you put the matter in my charge—"

"Who knows, Strock? Let us wait a while! Let us wait!"

Matters stood thus when, on the morning of June fifteenth, my old servant brought me a letter from the letter-carrier, a registered letter for which I had to sign. I looked at the address. I did not know the handwriting. The postmark, dating from two days before, was stamped at the post office of Morganton.

Morganton! Here at last was, no doubt, news from Mr. Elias Smith.

"Yes!" exclaimed I, speaking to my old servant, for lack of another, "it must be from Mr. Smith at last. I know no one else in Morganton. And if he writes he has news!"

"Morganton?" said the old woman, "isn't that the place where the demons set fire to their mountain?"

"Exactly."

"Oh, sir! I hope you don't mean to go back there!"

"Why not?"

"Because you will end by being burned up in that furnace of the Great Eyrie. And I wouldn't want you buried that way, sir."

"Cheer up, and let us see if it is not better news than that."

The envelope was sealed with red sealing wax, and stamped with a sort of coat of arms, surmounted with three stars. The paper was thick and very strong. I broke the envelope and drew out a letter. It was a single sheet, folded in four, and written on one side only. My first glance was for the signature.

There was no signature! Nothing but three initials at the end of the last line!

"The letter is not from the Mayor of Morganton," said I.

"Then from whom?" asked the old servant, doubly curious in her quality as a woman and as an old gossip.

Looking again at the three initials of the signature, I said, "I know no one for whom these letters would stand; neither at Morganton nor elsewhere."

The handwriting was bold. Both up strokes and down strokes very sharp, about twenty lines in all. Here is the letter, of which I, with good reason, retained an exact copy. It was dated, to my extreme stupefaction, from that mysterious Great Eyrie:

"Great Eyrie, Blue Ridge Mtns,
North Carolina, June 13th.
"To Mr. Strock:
Chief Inspector of Police
34 Long St., Washington, D.C.
"Sir,
"You were charged with the mission of penetrating the Great Eyrie.
"You came on April the twenty-eighth, accompanied by the Mayor of Morganton and two guides.

"You mounted to the foot of the wall, and you encircled it, finding it too high and steep to climb.

"You sought a breech and you found none.

"Know this: none enter the Great Eyrie; or if one enters, he never returns.

"Do not try again, for the second attempt will not result as did the first, but will have grave consequences for you.

"Heed this warning, or evil misfortune will come to you.

"M. O. W."

Chapter 7

A Third Machine

I confess that at first this letter dumbfounded me. "Ohs!" and "Ahs!" slipped from my open mouth. The old servant stared at me, not knowing what to think.

"Oh, sir! Is it bad news?"

I answered—for I kept few secrets from this faithful soul—by reading her the letter from end to end. She listened with much anxiety.

"A joke, without doubt," said I, shrugging my shoulders.

"Well," returned my superstitious handmaid, "if it isn't from the devil, it's from the devil's country, anyway."

Left alone, I again went over this unexpected letter. Reflection inclined me yet more strongly to believe that it was the work of a practical joker. My adventure was well known. The newspapers had given it in full detail. Some satirist, such as exists even in America, must have written this threatening letter to mock me.

To assume, on the other hand, that the Eyrie really served as the refuge of a band of criminals, seemed absurd. If they feared that the police would discover their retreat, surely they would not have been so foolish as thus to force attention upon themselves. Their chief security would lie in keeping their presence there unknown. They must have realized that such a challenge from them would only arouse the police to renewed activity. Dynamite or melinite would soon open an entrance to their fortress. Moreover, how could these men have, themselves, gained entrance into the Eyrie—unless there existed a passage which we had failed to discover? Assuredly the letter came from a jester or a madman; and I need not worry over it, nor even consider it.

Hence, though for an instant I had thought of showing this letter to Mr. Ward, I decided not to do so. Surely he would attach no importance to it. However, I did not destroy it, but locked it in my desk for safekeeping. If more letters came of the same kind, and with the same initials, I would attach as little weight to them as to this.

Several days passed quietly. There was nothing to lead me to expect that I should soon quit Washington; though in my line of duty one is never certain of the morrow. At any moment I might be sent speeding from Oregon to Florida, from Maine to Texas. And—this unpleasant thought haunted me frequently—if my next mission were no more successful than that to the Great Eyrie, I might as well give up and hand in my resignation from the force. Of the mysterious chauffeur or chauffeurs, nothing more was heard. I knew that our own government agents, as well as foreign ones, were keeping keen watch over all the roads and rivers, all the lakes and coasts of America. Of course, the size of the country made any close supervision impossible; but these twin inventors had not before chosen secluded and unfrequented spots in which to appear. The main highway of Wisconsin on a great race day, the harbor of Boston, incessantly crossed by thousands of boats, these were hardly what would be called hiding places! If the daring driver had not perished—of which there was always strong probability; then he must have left America. Perhaps he was in the waters of the Old World, or else resting in some retreat known only to himself, and in that case—

"Ah!" I repeated to myself, many times. "For such a retreat, as secret as inaccessible, this fantastic personage could not find one better than the Great Eyrie!" But, of course, a boat could not get there, any more than an automobile. Only high-flying birds of prey, eagles or condors, could find refuge there.

The nineteenth of June I was going to the police bureau, when, on leaving my house, I noticed two men who looked at me with a certain keenness. Not knowing them, I took no notice; and if my attention was drawn to the matter, it was because my servant spoke of it when I returned.

For some days, she said, she had noticed that two men seemed to be spying upon me in the street. They stood constantly, perhaps a hundred steps from my house; and she suspected that they followed me each time I went up the street.

"You are sure?" I asked.

"Yes, sir, and no longer ago than yesterday, when you came into the house, these men came slipping along in your footsteps, and then went away as soon as the door was shut behind you."

"You must be mistaken?"

"I am not, sir."

"And if you met these two men, you would know them?"

"I would."

"Good," I cried, laughing, "I see you have the very spirit for a detective. I must engage you as a member of our force."

"Joke if you like, sir. But I have still two good eyes, and I don't need spectacles to recognize people. Someone is spying on you, that's certain; and you should put some of your men to track them in turn."

"All right; I promise to do so," I said, to satisfy her. "And when my men get after them, we shall soon know what these mysterious fellows want of me."

In truth I did not take the good soul's excited announcement very seriously. I added, however, "When I go out, I will watch the people around me with great care."

"That will be best, sir."

My poor old housekeeper was always frightening herself at nothing. "If I see them again," she added, "I will warn you before you set foot out of doors."

"Agreed!" And I broke off the conversation, knowing well that if I allowed her to run on, she would end by being sure that Beelzebub himself and one of his chief attendants were at my heels.

The two following days, there was certainly no one spying on me, either at my exits or entrances. So I concluded my old servant had made much of nothing, as usual. But on the morning of the twenty-second of June, after rushing upstairs as rapidly as her age would permit, the devoted old soul burst into my room and in a half whisper gasped "Sir! Sir!"

"What is it?"

"They are there!"

"Who?" I queried, my mind on anything but the web she had been spinning about me.

"The two spies!"

"Themselves! In the street! Right in front of our windows! Watching the house, waiting for you to go out."

I went to the window and raising just an edge of the shade, so as not to give any warning, I saw two men on the pavement.

They were rather fine-looking men, broad-shouldered and vigorous, aged somewhat under forty, dressed in the ordinary fashion of the day, with slouched hats, heavy woolen suits, stout walking shoes and sticks in hand. Undoubtedly, they were staring persistently at my apparently unwatchful house. Then, having exchanged a few words, they strolled off a little way, and returned again.

"Are you sure these are the same men you saw before?"

"Yes, sir."

Evidently, I could no longer dismiss her warning as an hallucination; and I promised myself to clear up the matter. As to following the men myself, I was presumably too well known to them. To address them directly would probably be of no use. But that very day, one of our best men should be put on watch, and if the spies returned on the morrow, they should be tracked in their turn, and watched until their identity was established.

At the moment, were they waiting to follow me to police headquarters? For it was there that I was bound, as usual. If they accompanied me I might be able to offer them a hospitality for which they would scarce thank me.

I took my hat; and while the housekeeper remained peeping from the window, I went downstairs, opened the door, and stepped into the street.

The two men were no longer there.

Despite all my watchfulness that day I saw no more of them as I passed along the streets. From that time on, indeed, neither my old servant nor I saw them again before the house, nor did I encounter them elsewhere. Their appearance, however, was stamped upon my memory. I would not forget them.

Perhaps after all, admitting that I had been the object of their espionage, they had been mistaken in my identity. Having obtained a good look at me, they now followed me no more. So in the end, I came to regard this matter as of no more importance than the letter with the initials M. O. W.

Then, on the twenty-fourth of June, there came a new event, to further stimulate both my interest and that of the general public in the previous mysteries of the automobile and the boat. The Washington *Evening Star* published the following account, which was next morning copied by every paper in the country.

"Lake Kirdall in Kansas, forty miles west of Topeka, is little known. It deserves wider knowledge, and doubtless will have it hereafter, for attention is now drawn to it in a very remarkable way.

"This lake, deep among the mountains, appears to have no outlet. What it loses by evaporation, it regains from the little neighboring streamlets and the heavy rains.

"Lake Kirdall covers about seventy-five square miles, and its level is but slightly below that of the heights which surround it. Shut in among the mountains, it can be reached only by narrow and rocky gorges. Several villages, however, have sprung up upon its banks. It is full of fish, and fishing boats cover its waters.

"Lake Kirdall is in many places fifty feet deep

close to shore. Sharp, pointed rocks form the edges of this huge basin. Its surges, roused by high winds, beat upon its banks with fury, and the houses near at hand are often deluged with spray as if with the downpour of a hurricane. The lake, already deep at the edge, becomes yet deeper toward the center, where in some places soundings show over three hundred feet of water.

"The fishing industry supports a population of several thousands, and there are several hundred fishing boats in addition to the dozen or so of little steamers which serve the traffic of the lake. Beyond the circle of the mountains lie the railroads which transport the products of the fishing industry throughout Kansas and the neighboring states.

"This account of Lake Kirdall is necessary for the understanding of the remarkable facts which we are about to report."

And this is what the *Evening Star* then reported in its startling article: "For some time past, the fishermen have noticed a strange upheaval in the waters of the lake. Sometimes it rises as if a wave surged up from its depths. Even in perfectly calm weather, where there is no wind whatever, this upheaval sometimes arises in a mass of foam.

"Tossed about by violent waves and unaccountable currents, boats have been swept beyond all control. Sometimes they have been dashed one against another, and serious damage has resulted.

"This confusion of the waters evidently has its

origin somewhere in the depths of the lake; and various explanations have been offered to account for it. At first, it was suggested that the trouble was due to seismic forces, to some volcanic action beneath the lake; but this hypothesis had to be rejected when it was recognized that the disturbance was not confined to one locality, but spread itself over the entire surface of the lake, either at one part or another, in the center or along the edges, traveling along almost in a regular line and in a way to exclude entirely all idea of earthquake or volcanic action.

"Another hypothesis suggested that it was a marine monster who thus upheaved the waters. But unless the beast had been born in the lake and had there grown to its gigantic proportions unsuspected, which was scarce possible, he must have come there from outside. Lake Kirdall, however, has no connections with any other waters. If this lake were situated near any of the oceans, there might be subterranean canals; but in the center of America, and at the height of some thousands of feet above sea level, this is not possible. In short, here is another riddle not easy to solve, and it is much easier to point out the impossibility of false explanations, than to discover the true one.

"Is it possible that a submarine boat is being experimented with beneath the lake? Such boats are no longer impossible today. Some years ago, at Bridgeport, Connecticut, there was launched a boat, *The Protector*, which could go on the water, under the water, and also upon land. Built by an inventor named Lake, supplied with two motors, an electric one of seventy-five horse power, and a gasoline one of two hundred and fifty horse power, it was also provided with wheels a yard in diameter, which enabled it to roll over the roads, as well as swim the seas.

"But even then, granting that the turmoil of Lake Kirdall might be produced by a submarine, brought to a high degree of perfection, there remains as before the question how could it have reached Lake Kirdall? The lake, shut in on all sides by a circle of mountains, is no more accessible to a submarine than to a sea-monster.

"In whatever way this last puzzling question may be solved, the nature of this strange appearance can no longer be disputed since the twentieth of June. On that day, in the afternoon, the schooner *Markel* while speeding with all sails set, came into violent collision with something just below the water level. There was no shoal nor rock near; for the lake in this part is eighty or ninety feet deep. The schooner with both her bow and her side badly broken, ran great danger of sinking. She managed, however, to reach the shore before her decks were completely submerged.

"When the *Markel* had been pumped out and hauled up on shore, an examination showed that she had received a blow near the bow as if from a powerful ram.

"From this it seems evident that there is actually a submarine boat which darts about beneath the surface of Lake Kirdall with most remarkable rapidity.

"The thing is difficult to explain. Not only is

there a question as to how did the submarine get there. But why is it there? Why does it never come to the surface? What reason has its owner for remaining unknown? Are other disasters to be expected from its reckless course?"

The article in the *Evening Star* closed with this truly striking suggestion: "After the mysterious automobile, came the mysterious boat. Now comes the mysterious submarine.

"Must we conclude that the three engines are due to the genius of the same inventor, and that the three vehicles are in truth but one?"

Chapter 8

At Any Cost

The suggestion of the *Star* came like a revelation. It was accepted everywhere. Not only were these three vehicles the work of the same inventor; they were the same machine!

It was not easy to see how the remarkable transformation could be practically accomplished from one means of locomotion to the other. How could an automobile become a boat, and yet more, a submarine? All the machine seemed to lack was the power of flying through the air.

Nevertheless, everything that was known of the three different machines, as to their size, their shape, their lack of odor or of steam, and above all their remarkable speed, seemed to imply their identity. The public, grown blase with so many excitements, found in this new marvel a stimulus to reawaken their curiosity.

The newspapers dwelt now chiefly on the importance of the invention. This new engine, whether in one vehicle or three, had given proofs of its power. What amazing proofs! The invention must be bought at any price. The United States government must purchase it at once for the use of the nation. Assuredly, the great European powers would stop at nothing to be beforehand with America, and gain possession of an engine so invaluable for military and naval use. What incalculable advantages would it give to any nation, both on land and sea! Its destructive powers could not even be estimated, until its qualities and limitations were better known. No amount of money would be too great to pay for the secret; America could not put her millions to better use.

But to buy the machine, it was necessary to find the inventor; and there seemed the chief difficulty. In vain was Lake Kirdall searched from end to end. Even its depths were explored with a sounding line without result. Must it be concluded that the submarine no longer lurked beneath its waters? But in that case, how had the boat gotten away? For that matter, how had it come? An insoluble problem!

The submarine was heard from no more,

neither in Lake Kirdall nor elsewhere. It had disappeared like the automobile from the roads, and like the boat from the shores of America. Several times in my interviews with Mr. Ward, we discussed this matter, which still filled his mind. Our men continued everywhere on the lookout, but as unsuccessfully as other agents.

On the morning of the twenty-seventh of June, I was summoned into the presence of Mr. Ward.

"Well, Strock," said he, "here is a splendid chance for you to get your revenge."

"Revenge for the Great Eyrie disappointment?"

"Of course."

"What chance?" asked I, not knowing if he spoke seriously, or in jest.

"Why, here," he answered. "Would not you like to discover the inventor of this three-fold machine?"

"I certainly should, Mr. Ward. Give me the order to take charge of the matter, and I will accomplish the impossible, in order to succeed. It is true, I believe it will be difficult."

"Undoubtedly, Strock. Perhaps even more difficult than to penetrate into the Great Eyrie."

It was evident that Mr. Ward was intent on rallying me about my unsuccess. He would not do that, I felt assured, out of mere unkindness. Perhaps then he meant to rouse my resolution. He knew me well; and realized that I would have given anything in the world to recoup my defeat. I waited quietly for new instructions.

Mr. Ward dropped his jesting and said to me

very generously, "I know, Strock, that you accomplished everything that depended on human powers; and that no blame attaches to you. But we face now a matter very different from that of the Great Eyrie. The day the government decides to force that secret, everything is ready. We have only to spend some thousands of dollars, and the road will be open."

"That is what I would urge."

"But at present," said Mr. Ward, shaking his head, "it is much more important to place our hands on this fantastic inventor, who so constantly escapes us. That is work for a detective, indeed; a master detective!"

"He has not been heard from again?"

"No; and though there is every reason to believe that he has been, and still continues, beneath the waters of Lake Kirdall, it has been impossible to find any trace of him anywhere around there. One would almost fancy he had the power of making himself invisible, this Proteus of a mechanic!"

"It seems likely," said I, "that he will never be seen until he wishes to be."

"True, Strock. And to my mind there is only one way of dealing with him, and that is to offer him such an enormous price that he cannot refuse to sell his invention."

Mr. Ward was right. Indeed, the government had already made the effort to secure speech with this hero of the day, than whom surely no human being has ever better merited the title. The press had widely spread the news, and this extraordinary individual must assuredly know what the government desired of him, and how completely he could name the terms he wished.

"Surely," added Mr. Ward, "this invention can be of no personal use to the man, that he should hide it from the rest of us. There is every reason why he should sell it. Can this unknown be already some dangerous criminal who, thanks to his machine, hopes to defy all pursuit?"

My chief then went on to explain that it had been decided to employ other means in search of the inventor. It was possible after all that he had perished with his machine in some dangerous maneuver. If so, the ruined vehicle might prove almost as valuable and instructive to the mechanical world as the man himself. But since the accident to the schooner *Markel* on Lake Kirdall, no news of him whatever had reached the police.

On this point Mr. Ward did not attempt to hide his disappointment and his anxiety. Anxiety, yes, for it was manifestly becoming more and more difficult for him to fulfill his duty of protecting the public. How could we arrest criminals, if they could flee from justice at such speed over both land and sea? How could we pursue them under the oceans? And when dirigible balloons should also have reached their full perfection, we would even have to chase men through the air! I asked myself if my colleagues and I would not find ourselves some day reduced to utter helplessness? If police officials, become a useless incumbrance, would be definitely discarded by society?

Here, there recurred to me the jesting letter I

had received a fortnight before, the letter which threatened my liberty and even my life. I recalled, also, the singular espionage of which I had been the subject. I asked myself if I had better mention these things to Mr. Ward. But they seemed to have absolutely no relation to the matter now in hand. The Great Eyrie affair had been definitely put aside by the government, since an eruption was no longer threatening. And they now wished to employ me upon this newer matter. I waited, then, to mention this letter to my chief at some future time, when it would be not so sore a joke to me.

Mr. Ward again took up our conversation. "We are resolved by some means to establish communications with this inventor. He has disappeared, it is true; but he may reappear at any moment, and in any part of the country. I have chosen you, Strock, to follow him the instant he appears. You must hold yourself ready to leave Washington on the moment. Do not quit your house, except to come here to headquarters each day; notify me, each time by telephone, when you start from home, and report to me personally the moment you arrive here."

"I will follow orders exactly, Mr. Ward," I answered. "But permit me one question. Ought I to act alone, or will it not be better to join with me—?"

"That is what I intend," said the chief, interrupting me. "You are to choose two of our men whom you think the best fitted."

"I will do so, Mr. Ward. And now, if some day or other I stand in the presence of our man, what am I to do with him?"

"Above all things, do not lose sight of him. If there is no other way, arrest him. You shall have a warrant."

"A useful precaution, Mr. Ward. If he started to jump into his automobile and to speed away at the rate we know of, I must stop him at any cost. One cannot argue long with a man making two hundred miles an hour!"

"You must prevent that, Strock. And the arrest made; telegraph me. After that, the matter will be in my hands."

"Count on me, Mr. Ward; at any hour, day or night, I shall be ready to start with my men. I thank you for having entrusted this mission to me. If it succeeds, it will be a great honor—"

"And of great profit," added my chief, dismissing me.

Returning home, I made all preparations for a trip of indefinite duration. Perhaps my good housekeeper imagined that I planned to return to the Great Eyrie, which she regarded as an ante-chamber of hell itself. She said nothing, but went about her work with a most despairing face. Nevertheless, sure as I was of her discretion, I told her nothing. In this great mission I would confide in no one.

My choice of the two men to accompany me was easily made. They both belonged to my own department, and had many times under my direct command given proofs of their vigor, courage and intelligence. One, John Hart, of

Illinois was a man of thirty years; the other, aged thirty-two, was Nab Walker, of Massachusetts. I could not have had better assistants.

Several days passed, without news, either of the automobile, the boat, or the submarine. There were rumors in plenty, but the police knew them to be false. As to the reckless stories that appeared in the newspapers, they had most of them, no foundation whatever. Even the best journals cannot be trusted to refuse an exciting bit of news on the mere ground of its unreliability.

Then, twice in quick succession, there came what seemed trustworthy reports of the "man of the hour." The first asserted that he had been seen on the roads of Arkansas, near Little Rock. The second, that he was in the very middle of Lake Superior.

Unfortunately, these two notices were absolutely unreconcilable; for while the first gave the afternoon of June twenty-sixth, as the time of appearance, the second set it for the evening of the same day. Now, these two points of the United States territory are not less than eight hundred miles apart. Even granting the automobile this unthinkable speed, greater than any it had yet shown, how could it have crossed all the intervening country unseen? How could it traverse the states of Arkansas, Missouri, Iowa and Wisconsin, from end to end without any one of our agents giving us warning, without any interested person rushing to a telephone?

After these two momentary appearances, if appearances they were, the machine again dropped out of knowledge. Mr. Ward did not think it worthwhile to dispatch me and my men to either point whence it had been reported.

Yet since this marvelous machine seemed still in existence, something must be done. The following official notice was published in every newspaper of the United States under July 3rd. It was couched in the most formal terms.

"During the month of April, of the present year, an automobile traversed the roads of Pennsylvania, of Kentucky, of Ohio, of Tennessee, of Missouri, of Illinois; and, on the twenty-seventh of May, during the race held by the American Automobile Club, it covered the course in Wisconsin. Then it disappeared.

"During the first week of June, a boat maneuvering at great speed appeared off the coast of New England between Cape Cod and Cape Sable, and more particularly around Boston. Then it disappeared.

"In the second fortnight of the same month, a submarine boat was run beneath the waters of Lake Kirdall, in Kansas. Then it disappeared.

"Everything points to the belief that the same inventor must have built these three machines, or perhaps that they are the same machine, constructed so as to travel both on land and water.

"A proposition is therefore addressed to the said inventor, whoever he be, with the aim of acquiring the said machine.

"He is requested to make himself known and to name the terms upon which he will treat with the United States government. He is also requested to answer as promptly as possible to the Department of Federal Police, Washington D.C., United States of America.''

Such was the notice printed in large type on the front page of every newspaper. Surely it could not fail to reach the eye of him for whom it was intended, wherever he might be. He would read it. He could scarce fail to answer it in some manner. And why should he refuse such an unlimited offer? We had only to await his reply.

One can easily imagine how high the public curiosity rose. From morning till night, an eager and noisy crowd pressed about the bureau of police, awaiting the arrival of a letter or a telegram. The best reporters were on the spot. What honor, what profit would come to the paper which was first to publish the famous news! To know at last the name and place of the undiscoverable unknown! And to know if he would agree to some bargain with the government! It goes without saying that America does things on a magnicent scale. Millions would not be lacking for the inventor. If necessary all the millionaires in the country would open their inexhaustible purses!

The day passed. To how many excited and impatient people it seemed to contain more than twenty-four hours! And each hour held far more than sixty minutes! There came no answer, no letter, no telegram! The night following, there was still no news. And it was the same the next day—and the next.

There came, however, another result, which had been fully foreseen. The cables informed

Europe of what the United States government had done. The different powers of the Old World hoped also to obtain possession of the wonderful invention. Why should they not struggle for an advantage so tremendous? Why should they not enter the contest with their millions?

In brief, every great power took part in the affair—France, England, Russia, Italy, Austria, Germany. Only the states of the second order refrained from entering, with their smaller resources, upon a useless effort. The European press published notices identical with that of the United States. The extraordinary "chauffeur" had only to speak, to become a rival to the Vanderbilts, the Astors, the Goulds, the Morgans, and the Rothschilds of every country of Europe.

And, when the mysterious inventor made no sign, what attractive offers were held forth to tempt him to discard the secrecy in which he was enwrapped! The whole world became a public market, an auction house whence arose the most amazing bids. Twice a day the newspapers would add up the amounts, and these kept rising from millions to millions. The end came when the United States Congress, after a memorable session, voted to offer the sum of twenty million dollars. And there was not a citizen of the states of whatever rank, who objected to the amount, so much importance was attached to the possession of this prodigious engine of locomotion. As for me, I said emphatically to my old housekeeper: "The machine is worth even more than that."

Evidently the other nations of the world did not think so, for their bids remained below the final sum. But how useless was this mighty struggle of the great rivals! He had never existed! It was all a monstrous pretense of the American newspapers. That, at least, became the announced view of the Old World.

And so the time passed. There was no further news of our man, there was no response from him. He appeared no more. For my part, not knowing what to think, I commenced to lose all hope of reaching any solution to the strange affair.

Then on the morning of the fifteenth of July a letter without postmark was found in the mail-box of the police bureau. After the authorities had studied it, it was given out to the Washington journals, which published it in facsimile, in special numbers. It was couched as follows:

Chapter 9

The Second Letter

"On Board the Terror

"July 15.

"To the Old and New World,

"The propositions emanating from the different governments of Europe, as also that which has finally been made by the United States of America, need expect no other answer than this:

"I refuse absolutely and definitely the sums offered for my invention.

"My machine will be neither French nor German, nor Austrian nor Russian, nor English nor American.

"The invention will remain my own, and I shall use it as pleases me.

"With it, I hold control of the entire world, and there lies no force within the reach of humanity which is able to resist me, under any circumstances whatsoever.

"Let no one attempt to seize or stop me. It is, and will be, utterly impossible. Whatever injury anyone attempts against me, I will return a hundredfold.

"As to the money which is offered me, I despise it! I have no need of it. Moreover, on the day when it pleases me to have millions, or billions, I have but to reach out my hand and take them.

"Let both the Old and the New World realize this: They can accomplish nothing against me; I can accomplish anything against them.

"So I sign this letter:

"The Master of the World."

Chapter 10

Outside the Law

Such was the letter addressed to the government of the United States. As to the person who had placed it in the mailbox of the police, no one had seen him.

The sidewalk in front of our offices had probably not been vacant during the entire night. From sunset to sunrise, there had always been people, busy, anxious, or curious, passing before our door. It is true, however, that even then, the bearer of the letter might easily have slipped by unseen and dropped the letter in the box. The night had been so dark, you could scarcely see from one side of the street to the other.

I have said that this letter appeared in facsimile in all the newspapers to which the government communicated it. Perhaps one would naturally imagine that the first comment of the public would be, "This is the work of some practical joker." It was in that way that I had accepted my letter from the Great Eyrie, five weeks before.

But this was not the general attitude toward the present letter, neither in Washington, nor in the rest of America. To the few who would have maintained that the document should not be taken seriously, an immense majority would have responded. "This letter has not the style nor the spirit of a jester. Only one man could have written it; and that is the inventor of this unapproachable machine."

To the people this conclusion seemed indisputable owing to a curious state of mind easily explainable. For all the strange facts of which the key had hitherto been lacking, this letter furnished an explanation. The theory now almost universally accepted was as follows. The inventor had hidden himself for a time, only in order to reappear more startlingly in some new light. Instead of having perished in an accident, he had concealed himself in some retreat where the police were unable to discover him. Then to assert positively his attitude toward all governments he had written this letter.

But instead of dropping it in the post in any one locality, which might have resulted in its being traced to him, he had come to Washington and deposited it himself in the very spot suggested by the government's official notice, the bureau of police.

Well! If this remarkable personage had reckoned that this new proof of his existence would make some noise in two worlds, he certainly figured rightly. That day, the millions of good folk who read and re-read their daily paper could—to employ a well-known phrase—scarcely believe their eyes.

As for myself, I studied carefully every phrase of the defiant document. The handwriting was black and heavy. An expert at chirography would doubtless have distinguished in the lines traces of a violent temperament, of a character stern and unsocial. Suddenly, a cry escaped me—a cry that fortunately my housekeeper did not hear. Why had I not noticed sooner the resemblance of the handwriting to that of the letter I had received from Morganton?

Moreover, a yet more significant coincidence, the initials with which my letter had been signed, did they not stand for the words "Master of the World?"

And whence came the second letter? "On Board the Terror." Doubtless this name was that of the triple machine commanded by the mysterious captain. The initials in my letter were his own signature; and it was he who had threatened me, if I dared to renew my attempt on the Great Eyrie.

I rose and took from my desk the letter of June thirteenth. I compared it with the facsimile in the newspapers. There was no doubt about it. They were both in the same peculiar handwriting.

My mind worked eagerly. I sought to trace the probable deductions from this striking fact, known only to myself. The man who had threatened me was the commander of the Terror—startling name, only too well justified! I asked myself if our search could not now be prosecuted under less vague conditions. Could we not now start our men upon a trail which would lead definitely to success? In short, what relation existed between the Terror and the Great Eyrie? What connection was there between the phenomena of the Blue Ridge Mountains, and the no less phenomenal performances of the fantastic machine?

I knew what my first step should be; and with the letter in my pocket, I hastened to police headquarters. Inquiring if Mr. Ward was within and receiving an affirmative reply, I hastened toward his door, and rapped upon it with unusual and perhaps unnecessary vigor. Upon his call to enter, I stepped eagerly into the room.

The chief had spread before him the letter published in the papers, not a facsimile, but the original itself which had been deposited in the letter-box of the department.

"You come as if you had important news, Strock?"

"Judge for yourself, Mr. Ward;" and I drew from my pocket the letter with the initials.

Mr. Ward took it, glanced at its face, and asked, "What is this?"

"A letter signed only with initials, as you can see."

"And where was it posted?"

"In Morganton, in North Carolina."

"When did you receive it?"

"A month ago, the thirteenth of June."

"What did you think of it then?"

"That it had been written as a joke."

"And—now—Strock?"

"I think what you will think, Mr. Ward, after you have studied it."

My chief turned to the letter again and read it carefully. "It is signed with three initials," said he.

"Yes, Mr. Ward, and those initials belong to the words, 'Master of the World,' in this facsimile."

"Of which this is the original," responded Mr. Ward, taking it up.

"It is quite evident," I urged, "that the two letters are by the same hand."

"It seems so."

"You see what threats are made against me, to protect the Great Eyrie."

"Yes, the threat of death! But Strock, you have had this letter for a month. Why have you not shown it to me before?"

"Because I attached no importance to it. Today, after the letter from the Terror, it must be taken seriously."

"I agree with you. It appears to me most important. I even hope it may prove the means of tracking this strange personage."

"That is what I also hope, Mr. Ward."

"Only—what connection can possibly exist between the Terror and the Great Eyrie?"

"That I do not know. I cannot even imagine—"

"There can be but one explanation," continued Mr. Ward, "though it is almost inadmissible, even impossible."

"And that is?"

"That the Great Eyrie was the spot selected by the inventor, where he gathered his material."

"That is impossible!" cried I. "In what way would he get his material in there? And how get his machine out? After what I have seen, Mr. Ward, your suggestion is impossible."

"Unless, Strock—"

"Unless what?" I demanded.

"Unless the machine of this Master of the World has also wings, which permit it to take refuge in the Great Eyrie."

At the suggestion that the Terror, which had searched the deeps of the sea, might be capable also of rivaling the vultures and the eagles, I could not restrain an expressive shrug of incredulity. Neither did Mr. Ward himself dwell upon the extravagant hypothesis.

He took the two letters and compared them afresh. He examined them under a microscope, especially the signatures, and established their perfect identity. Not only the same hand, but the same pen had written them.

After some moments of further reflection, Mr. Ward said, "I will keep your letter, Strock. Decidedly, I think, that you are fated to play an important part in this strange affair—or rather in these two affairs. What thread attaches them, I cannot yet see; but I am sure the thread exists. You have been connected with the first, and it will not be surprising if you have a large part in the second.''

''I hope so, Mr. Ward. You know how inquisitive I am.''

''I do, Strock. That is understood. Now, I can only repeat my former order; hold yourself in readiness to leave Washington at a moment's warning.''

All that day, the public excitement caused by the defiant letter mounted steadily higher. It was felt both at the White House and at the Capitol that public opinion absolutely demanded some action. Of course, it was difficult to do anything. Where could one find this Master of the World? And even if he were discovered, how could he be captured? He had at his disposal not only the powers he had displayed, but apparently still greater resources as yet unknown. How had he been able to reach Lake Kirdall over the rocks; and how had he escaped from it? Then, if he had indeed appeared on Lake Superior, how had he covered all the intervening territory unseen?

What a bewildering affair it was altogether! This, of course, made it all the more important to get to the bottom of it. Since the millions of dollars had been refused, force must be employed. The inventor and his invention were not to be bought. And in what haughty and menacing terms he had couched his refusal! So be it! He must be treated as an enemy of society, against whom all means became justified, that he might be deprived of his power to injure others. The idea that he had perished was now entirely discarded. He was alive, very much alive; and his existence constituted a perpetual public danger!

Influenced by these ideas, the government issued the following proclamation:

"Since the commander of the Terror has refused to make public his invention at any price whatever, since the use which he makes of his machine constitutes a public menace, against which it is impossible to guard, the said commander of the Terror is hereby placed beyond the protection of the law. Any measures taken in the effort to capture or destroy either him or his machine will be approved and rewarded."

It was a declaration of war, war to the death against this "Master of the World" who thought to threaten and defy an entire nation, the American nation!

Before the day was over, various rewards of large amounts were promised to anyone who revealed the hiding place of this dangerous inventor, to anyone who could identify him, and to anyone who should rid the country of him.

Such was the situation during the last fortnight of July. All was left to the hazard of fortune. The moment the outlaw reappeared he would be seen and signaled, and when the chance came he would be arrested. This could not be accomplished when he was in his automobile on land or in his boat on the water. No; he must be seized suddenly, before he had any opportunity to escape by means of that speed which no other machine could equal.

I was therefore all alert, awaiting an order from Mr. Ward to start out with my men. But the order did not arrive for a very good reason that the man whom it concerned remained undiscovered. The end of July approached. The newspapers continued the excitement. They published repeated rumors. New clues were constantly being announced. But all this was mere idle talk. Telegrams reached the police bureau from every part of America, each contradicting and nullifyng the others. The enormous rewards offered could not help but lead to accusations, errors, and blunders, made, many of them, in good faith. One time it would be a cloud of dust, which must have contained the automobile. At another time, almost any wave on any of America's thousand lakes represented the submarine. In truth, in the excited state of the public imagination, apparitions assailed us from every side.

At last, on the twenty-ninth of July, I received a telephone message to come to Mr. Ward on the instant.

"You leave in an hour, Strock," said he

"Where for?"

"For Toledo."

"It has been seen?"

"Yes. At Toledo you will get your final orders."

"In an hour, my men and I will be on the way."

"Good! And, Strock, I now give you a formal order."

"What is it, Mr. Ward?"

"To succeed—this time to succeed!"

Chapter 11
The Campaign

So the undiscoverable commander had reappeared upon the territory of the United States! He had never shown himself in Europe either on the roads or in the seas. He had not crossed the Atlantic, which apparently he could have traversed in three days. Did he then intend to make only America the scene of his exploits? Ought we to conclude from this that he was an American?

Let me insist upon this point. It seemed clear that the submarine might easily have crossed the vast sea which separates the New and the Old World. Not only would its amazing speed have made its voyage short, in comparison to that of the swiftest steamship, but also it would have escaped all the storms that make the voyage dangerous. Tempests did not exist for it. It had but to abandon the surface of the waves, and it could find absolute calm a few score feet beneath.

But the inventor had not crossed the Atlantic, and if he were to be captured now, it would probably be in Ohio, since Toledo is a city of that state.

This time the fact of the machine's appearance had been kept secret, between the police and the agent who had warned them, and whom I was hurrying to meet. No journal—and many would have paid high for the chance—was printing this news. We had decided that nothing should be revealed until our effort was at an end. No indiscretion would be committed by either my comrades or myself.

The man to whom I was sent with an order from Mr. Ward was named Arthur Wells. He awaited us at Toledo. The city of Toledo stands at the western end of Lake Erie. Our train sped during the night across West Virginia and Ohio. There was no delay; and before noon the next day the locomotive stopped in the Toledo depot.

John Hart, Nab Walker and I stepped out with traveling bags in our hands, and revolvers in our pockets. Perhaps we should need weapons for an attack, or even to defend ourselves. Scarcely had I stepped from the train when I picked out the man who awaited us. He was scanning the arriving passengers impatiently, evidently as eager and full of haste as I.

I approached him. "Mr. Wells?" said I.

"Mr. Strock?" asked he.

"Yes."

"I am at your command," said Mr. Wells.

"Are we to stop any time in Toledo?" I asked.

"No; with your permission, Mr. Strock. A

carriage with two good horses is waiting outside the station; and we must leave at once to reach our destination as soon as possible.''

''We will go at once,'' I answered, signing to my two men to follow us. ''Is it far?''

''Twenty miles.''

''And the place is called?''

''Black Rock Creek.''

Having left our bags at a hotel, we started on our drive. Much to my surprise I found there were provisions sufficient for several days packed beneath the seat of the carriage. Mr. Wells told me that the region around Black Rock Creek was among the wildest in the state. There was nothing there to attract either farmers or fishermen. We would find not an inn for our meals nor a room in which to sleep. Fortunately, during the July heat there would be no hardship even if we had to lie one or two nights under the stars.

More probably, however, if we were successful, the matter would not occupy us many hours. Either the commander of the Terror would be surprised before he had a chance to escape, or he would take to flight and we must give up all hope of arresting him.

I found Arthur Wells to be a man of about forty, large and powerful. I knew him by reputation to be one of the best of our local police agents. Cool in danger and enterprising always, he had proven his daring on more than one occasion at the peril of his life. He had been in Toledo on a wholly different mission, when chance had thrown him on the track of the Terror.

We drove rapidly along the shore of Lake Erie, toward the southwest. This inland sea of water is on the northern boundary of the United States, lying between Canada on one side and the states of Ohio, Pennsylvania and New York on the other. If I stop to mention the geographical position of this lake, its depth, its extent, and the waters nearest around, it is because the knowledge is necessary for the understanding of the events which were about to happen.

The surface of Lake Erie covers about ten thousand square miles. It is nearly six hundred feet above sea level. It is joined on the northwest, by means of the Detroit River, with the still greater lakes to the westward, and receives their waters. It has also rivers of its own though of less importance, such as the Rocky, the Cuyahoga, and the Black. The lake empties at its northeastern end into Lake Ontario by means of Niagara River and its celebrated falls.

The greatest known depth of Lake Erie is over one hundred and thirty feet. Hence it will be seen that the mass of its waters is considerable. In short, this is a region of most magnificent lakes. The land, though not situated far northward, is exposed to the full sweep of the Arctic cold. The region to the northward is low, and the winds of winter rush down with extreme violence. Hence Lake Erie is sometimes frozen over from shore to shore.

The principal cities on the borders of this great lake are Buffalo at the east, which belongs to New York State, and Toledo in Ohio, at the west, with Cleveland and Sandusky, both Ohio cities, at the south. Smaller towns and villages are numerous along the shore. The traffic is naturally large, its annual value being estimated at considerably over two million dollars.

Our carriage followed a rough and little used road along the borders of the lake; and as we toiled along, Arthur Wells told me what he had learned.

Less than two days before, on the afternoon of July twenty-seventh, Wells had been riding on horseback toward the town of Herly. Five miles outside the town, he was riding through a little wood, when he saw, far up across the lake, a submarine which rose suddenly above the waves. He stopped, tied his horse, and stole on foot to the edge of the lake. There, from behind a tree he had seen—with his own eyes seen—this submarine advance toward him, and stop at the mouth of Black Rock Creek. Was it the famous machine for which the whole world was seeking, which thus came directly to his feet?

When the submarine was close to the rocks, two men climbed out upon its deck and stepped ashore. Was one of them this Master of the World, who had not been seen since he was reported from Lake Superior? Was this the mysterious Terror which had thus risen from the depths of Lake Erie?

"I was alone," said Wells. "Alone on the edge of the Creek. If you and your assistants, Mr. Strock, had been there, we four against two, we would have been able to reach these men and seize them before they could have regained their boat and fled."

"Probably," I answered. "But were there no others on the boat with them? Still, if we had seized the two, we could at least have learned who they were."

"And above all," added Wells, "if one of them turned out to be the captain of the Terror!"

"I have only one fear, Wells; this submarine, whether it is one we seek or another, may have left the creek since your departure."

"We shall know about that in a few hours, now. Pray Heaven they are still there! Then when night comes—"

"But," I asked, "did you remain watching in the wood until night?"

"No; I left after an hour's watching, and rode straight for the telegraph station at Toledo. I reached there late at night and sent immediate word to Washington."

"That was the night before last. Did you return yesterday to Black Rock Creek?"

"Yes."

"The submarine was still there?"

"In the same spot."

"And the two men?"

"The same two men. I judge that some accident had happened, and they came to this lonely spot to repair it."

"Probably so," said I. "Some damage which made it impossible for them to regain their usual hiding place. If only they are still here!"

"I have reason to believe they will be, for quite a lot of stuff was taken out of the boat, and laid about upon the shore; and as well as I could discern from a distance they seemed to be working on board."

"Only the two men?"

"Only the two."

"But," protested I, "can two be sufficient to handle an apparatus of such speed, and of such intricacy, as to be at once an automobile, boat and submarine?"

"I think not, Mr. Strock; but I only saw the same two. Several times they came to the edge of the little wood where I was hidden, and gathered sticks for a fire which they made upon the beach. The region is so uninhabited and the creek so hidden from the lake that they ran little danger of discovery. They seemed to know this."

"You would recognize them both again?"

"Perfectly. One was of middle size, vigorous, and quick of movement, heavily bearded. The other was smaller, but stocky and strong. Yesterday, as before, I left the wood about five o'clock and hurried back to Toledo. There I found a telegraph from Mr. Ward, notifying me of your coming; and I awaited you at the station."

Summed up, then, the news amounted to this: For forty hours past a submarine, presumably the one we sought, had been hidden in Black Rock Creek, engaged in repairs. Probably these were absolutely necessary, and we should find the boat still there. As to how the Terror came to be in Lake Erie, Arthur Wells and I discussed that, and agreed that it was a very probable place for her. The last time she had been seen was on Lake Superior. From there to Lake Erie the machine could have come by the roads of Michigan, but since no one had remarked its passage and as both the police and the people were specially aroused and active in that portion of the country it seemed more probable, that the Terror had come by water. There was a clear route through the chain of the Great Lakes and their rivers, by which in her character of a submarine she could easily proceed undiscovered.

And now, if the Terror had already left the creek, or if she escaped when we attempted to seize her in what direction would she turn? In any case, there was little chance of following her. There were two torpedo-destroyers at the port of Buffalo, at the other extremity of Lake Erie.* Before I left Washington Mr. Ward had informed me of their presence; and a telegram to their commanders would, if there were need, start them in pursuit of the Terror. But despite their splendid speed, how could they vie with her! And if she plunged beneath the waters, they would be helpless. Moreover Arthur Wells averred that in case of a battle, the advantage would not be with the destroyers, despite their large crews, and many guns. Hence, if we did not succeed this night, the campaign would end in failure.

Arthur Wells knew Black Rock Creek thoroughly, having hunted there more than once. It was bordered in most places with sharp

* By treaty between the United States and Canada, there are no vessels of war whatever on the Great Lakes. These might, however, have been little launches belonging to the customs service.

rocks against which the waters of the lake beat heavily. Its channel was some thirty feet deep, so that the Terror could take shelter either upon the surface or under water. In two or three places the steep banks gave way to sand beaches which led to little gorges reaching up toward the woods, two or three hundred feet.

It was seven in the evening when our carriage reached these woods. There was still daylight enough for us to see easily, even in the shade of the trees. To have crossed openly to the edge of the creek would have exposed us to the view of the men of the Terror, if she were still there, and thus give her warning to escape.

"Had we better stop here?" I asked Wells, as our rig drew up to the edge of the woods.

"No, Mr. Strock," said he. "We had better leave the carriage deeper in the woods, where there will be no chance whatever of our being seen."

"Can the carriage drive under these trees?"

"It can," declared Wells. "I have already explored these woods thoroughly. Five or six hundred feet from here, there is a little clearing, where we will be completely hidden, and where our horses may find pasture. Then, as soon as it is dark, we will go down to the beach, at the edge of the rocks which shut the mouth of the creek. Thus if the Terror is still there, we shall stand between her and escape."

Eager as we all were for action, it was evidently best to do as Wells suggested and wait for night. The intervening time could well be occupied as he said. Leading the horses by the bridle, while they dragged the empty carriage, we proceeded through the heavy woods. The tall pines, the stalwart oaks, the cypress scattered here and there, made the evening darker overhead. Beneath our feet spread a carpet of scattered herbs, pine needles and dead leaves. Such was the thickness of the upper foliage that the last rays of the setting sun could no longer penetrate here. We had to feel our way; and it was not without some knocks that the carriage reached the clearing ten minutes later.

This clearing, surrounded by great trees, formed a sort of oval, covered with rich grass. Here it was still daylight, and the darkness would scarcely deepen for over an hour. There was thus time to arrange an encampment and to rest a while after our hard trip over the rough and rocky roads.

Of course, we were intensely eager to approach the Creek and see if the Terror was still there. But prudence restrained us. A little patience, and the night would enable us to reach a commanding position unsuspected. Wells urged this strongly; and despite my eagerness, I felt that he was right.

The horses were unharnessed, and left to browse under the care of the coachman who had driven us. The provisions were unpacked, and John Hart and Nab Walker spread out a meal on the grass at the foot of a superb cypress which recalled to me the forest odors of Morganton and Pleasant Garden. We were hungry and thirsty; and food and drink were not lacking. Then our pipes were lighted to calm the anxious moments of waiting that remained.

Silence reigned within the wood. The last song of the birds had ceased. With the coming of night the breeze fell little by little, and the leaves scarcely quivered even at the tops of the highest branches. The sky darkened rapidly after sundown and twilight deepened into obscurity.

I looked at my watch, it was half-past eight. "It is time, Wells."

"When you will, Mr. Strock."

"Then let us start."

We cautioned the coachman not to let the horses stray beyond the clearing. Then we started. Wells went in advance, I followed him, and John Hart and Nab Walker came behind. In the darkness, we three would have been helpless without the guidance of Wells. Soon we reached the farther border of the woods; and before us stretched the banks of Black Rock Creek.

All was silent; all seemed deserted. We could advance without risk. If the Terror was there, she had cast anchor behind the rocks. But was she there? That was the momentous question! As we approached the denouement of this exciting affair, my heart was in my throat.

Wells motioned to us to advance. The sand of the shore crushed beneath our steps. The two hundred feet between us and the mouth of the creek were crossed softly, and a few minutes sufficed to bring us to the rocks at the edge of the lake.

There was nothing! Nothing!

The spot where Wells had left the Terror twenty-four hours before was empty. The "Master of the World" was no longer at Black Rock Creek.

Chapter 12

Black Rock Creek

Human nature is prone to illusions. Of course, there had been all along a probability that the Terror had deserted the locality, even admitting that it was she Wells had seen the previous day. If some damage to her triple system of loco-motion had prevented her from regaining either by land or by water her usual hiding place, and obliged her to seek refuge in Black Rock Creek, what ought we to conclude now upon finding her here no longer? Obviously, that, having finished her repairs, she had continued on her way, and was already far beyond the water of Lake Erie.

But probable as this result had been from the first, we had more and more ignored it as our trip proceeded. We had come to accept as a fact that we should meet the Terror, that we should find her anchored at the base of the rocks where Wells had seen her.

And now what disappointment! I might even

say, what despair! All our efforts gone for nothing! Even if the Terror was still upon the lake, to find her, reach her and capture her, was beyond our power, and—it might as well be fully recognized—beyond all human power.

We stood there, Wells and I, completely crushed, while John Hart, and Nab Walker, no less chagrined, went tramping along the banks of the Creek, seeking any trace that had been left behind.

Posted there, at the mouth of the Creek, Wells and I exchanged scarcely a word. What need was there of words to enable us to understand each other! After our eagerness and our despair, we were now exhausted. Defeated in our well-planned attempt, we felt as unwilling to abandon our campaign, as we were unable to continue.

Nearly an hour slipped by. We could not resolve to leave the place. Our eyes still sought to pierce the night. Sometimes a glimmer, due to the sparkle of the waters, trembled on the surface of the lake. Then it vanished, and with it the foolish hope that it had roused. Sometimes again, we thought we saw a shadow outlined against the dark, the silhouette of an approaching boat. Yet again some eddies would swirl up at our feet, as if the Creek had been stirred within its depths. These vain imaginings were dissipated one after the other. They were but the illusions raised by our strained fancies.

At length our companions rejoined us. My first question was, "Nothing new?"

"Nothing," said John Hart.

"You have explored both banks of the Creek?"

"Yes," responded Nab Walker, "as far as the shallow water above; and we have not seen even a vestige of the things which Mr. Wells saw laid on the shore."

"Let us wait awhile," said I, unable to resolve upon a return to the woods.

At that moment our attention was caught by a sudden agitation of the waters, which swelled upward at the foot of the rocks.

"It is like the swell from a vessel," said Wells.

"Yes," said I, instinctively lowering my voice. "What has caused it? The wind has completely died out. Does it come from something on the surface of the lake?"

"Or from something underneath," said Wells, bending forward, the better to determine.

The commotion certainly seemed as if caused by some boat, whether from beneath the water, or approaching the creek from outside upon the lake.

Silent, motionless, we strained our eyes and ears to pierce the profound obscurity. The faint noise of the waves of the lake lapping on the shore beyond the creek, came to us distinctly through the night. John Hart and Nab Walker drew a little aside upon a higher ridge of rocks. As for me, I leaned close to the water to watch the agitation. It did not lessen. On the contrary it became momentarily more evident, and I began to distinguish a sort of regular throbbing, like that produced by a screw in motion.

"There is no doubt," declared Wells, leaning close to me, "there is a boat coming toward us."

"There certainly is," responded I, "unless they have whales or sharks in Lake Erie."

"No, it is a boat," repeated Wells. "Is she headed toward the mouth of the creek, or is she going further up it?"

"This is just where you saw the boat twice before?"

"Yes, just here."

"Then if this is the same one, and it can be no other, she will probably return to the same spot."

"There!" whispered Wells, extending his hand toward the entrance of the creek.

Our companions rejoined us, and all four, crouching low upon the bank, peered in the direction he pointed.

We vaguely distinguished a black mass moving through the darkness. It advanced very slowly and was still outside the creek, upon the lake, perhaps a cable's length to the northeast. We could scarcely hear even now the faint throbbing of its engines. Perhaps they had stopped and the boat was only gliding forward under their previous impulse.

It seemed, then, that this was indeed the submarine which Wells had watched, and it was returning to pass this night like the last, within the shelter of the creek.

Why had it left the anchorage, if only to return? Had it suffered some new disaster, which again impaired its power? Or had it been before compelled to leave, with its repairs still unfinished? What cause constrained it to return here? Was there some imperious reason why it could no longer be turned into an automobile, and go darting away across the roads of Ohio?

To all these questions which came crowding upon me, I could give no answer. Furthermore both Wells and I kept reasoning under the assumption that this was really the Terror commanded by the "Master of the World" who had dated from it his letter of defiance to the government. Yet this premise was still unproven, no matter how confident we might feel of it.

Whatever boat this was, that stole so softly through the night it continued to approach us. Assuredly its captain must know perfectly the channels and shore of Black Rock Creek, since he ventured here in such darkness. Not a single ray from within the cabin glimmered through any crevice.

A moment later, we heard some machinery moving very softly. The swell of the eddies grew stronger, and in a few moments the boat touched the "quay."

This word "quay," only used in that region, exactly describes the spot. The rocks at our feet formed a level, five or six feet above the water, and descending to it perpendicularly, exactly like a landing wharf.

"We must not stop here," whispered Wells, seizing me by the arm.

"No," I answered, "they might see us. We must lie crouched upon the beach! Or we might hide in some crevice of the rocks."

"We will follow you."

There was not a moment to lose. The dark mass was now close at hand, and on its deck, but slightly raised above the surface of the water, we could trace the silhouettes of two men.

Were there, then, really only two on board?

We stole softly back to where the ravines rose toward the woods above. Several niches in the rocks were at hand. Wells and I crouched down in one, my two assistants in another. If the men on the Terror landed, they could not see us; but we could see them, and would be able to act as opportunity offered.

There were some slight noises from the boat, a few words exchanged in our own language. It was evident that the vessel was preparing to anchor. Then almost instantly, a rope was thrown out, exactly on the point of the quay where we had stood.

Leaning forward, Wells could discern that the rope was seized by one of the mariners, who had leaped ashore. Then we heard a grappling-iron scrape along the ground.

Some moments later, steps crunched upon the sand. Two men came up the ravine, and went onward toward the edge of the woods, guiding their steps by a ship lantern.

Where were they going? Was Black Rock Creek a regular hiding place of the Terror? Had her commander a depot here for stores or provisions? Did they come here to restock their craft, when the whim of their wild voyaging brought them to this part of the continent? Did they know this deserted, uninhabited spot so well, that they had no fear of ever being discovered here?

"What shall we do?" whispered Wells.

"Wait till they return, and then—" My words were cut short by a surprise. The men were not thirty feet from us, when, one of them chancing to turn suddenly, the light of their lantern fell full upon his face.

He was one of the two men who had watched before my house in Long Street. I could not be mistaken. I recognized him as positively as my old servant had done. It was he; it was assuredly one of the spies of whom I had never been able to find any further traces! There was no longer any doubt, my warning letter had come from them. It was therefore from the "Master of the World"; it had been written from the Terror; and this was the Terror. Once more I asked myself what could be the connection between this machine and the Great Eyrie!

In whispered words, I told Wells of my discovery. His only comment was, "It is all incomprehensible!"

Meanwhile the two men had continued on their way to the woods, and were gathering sticks beneath the trees. "What if they discover our encampment?" murmured Wells.

"No danger, if they do not go beyond the nearest trees."

"But if they do discover it?"

"They will hurry back to their boat, and we shall be able to cut off their retreat."

Toward the creek, where their craft lay, there was no further sound. I left my hiding place; I descended the ravine to the quay; I stood on the very spot where the grappling-iron was fast among the rocks.

The Terror lay there, quiet at the end of its cable. Not a light was on board; not a person visible, either on the deck, or on the bank. Was not this my opportunity? Should I leap on board and there await the return of the two men?

"Mr. Strock!" It was Wells, who called to me softly from close at hand.

I drew back in all haste and crouched down beside him. Was it too late to take possession of the boat? Or would the attempt perhaps result in disaster from the presence of others watching on board?

At any rate, the two men with the lantern were close at hand returning down the ravine. Plainly they suspected nothing. Each carrying a bundle of wood, they came forward and stopped upon the quay.

Then one of them raised his voice, though not loudly. "Hullo! Captain!"

"All right," answered a voice from the boat.

Wells murmured in my ear, "There are three!"

"Perhaps four," I answered, "perhaps five or six!"

The situation grew more complicated. Against a crew so numerous, what ought we to do? The least imprudence might cost us dear! Now that the two men had returned, would they re-embark with their fagots? Then would the boat leave the creek, or would it remain anchored until day? If it withdrew, would it not be lost to us? It could leave the waters of Lake Erie, and cross any of the neighboring states by land; or it could retrace its road by the Detroit River which would lead it to Lake Huron and the Great Lakes above. Would such an opportunity as this, in the narrow waters of Black Rock Creek, ever occur again!

"At least," said I to Wells, "we are four. They do not expect attack; they will be surprised. The result is in the hands of Providence."

I was about to call our two men, when Wells again seized my arm. "Listen!" said he.

One of the men hailed the boat, and it drew close up to the rocks. We heard the captain say to the two men ashore, "Everything is all right, up there?"

"Everything, Captain."

"There are still two bundles of wood left there?"

"Two."

"Then one more trip will bring them all on board the Terror."

The Terror! It was she!

"Yes; just one more trip," answered one of the men.

"Good; then we will start off again at daybreak."

Were there then but three of them on board? The captain, this Master of the World, and these two men?

Evidently they planned to take aboard the last of their wood. Then they would withdraw within their machine, and go to sleep. Would not that be the time to surprise them before they could defend themselves?

Rather than to attempt to reach and capture the ship in face of this resolute captain who was guarding it, Wells and I agreed that it was better to let his men return unassailed, and wait till they were all asleep.

It was now half an hour after ten. Steps were once more heard upon the shore. The man with a lantern and his companion, again remounted the ravine toward the woods. When they were safely beyond hearing. Wells went to warn our men, while I stole forward again to the very edge of the water.

The Terror lay at the end of a short cable. As well as I could judge, she was long and slim, shaped like a spindle, without chimney, without masts, without rigging, such a shape as had been described when she was seen on the coast of New England.

I returned to my place, with my men in the shelter of the ravine; and we looked to our revolvers, which might well prove of service.

Five minutes had passed since the men reached the woods, and we expected their return at any moment. After that, we must wait at least an hour before we made our attack; so that both the captain and his comrades might be deep in sleep. It was important that they should have not a moment either to send their craft darting out upon the waters of Lake Erie, or to plunge it beneath the waves where we would have been entrapped with it.

In all my career I have never felt such impatience. It seemed to me that the two men must have been detained in the woods. Something had barred their return.

Suddenly a loud noise was heard, the tumult of runaway horses, galloping furiously along the shore!

They were our own, which, frightened, and perhaps neglected by the driver, had broken away from the clearing, and now came rushing along the bank.

At the same moment, the two men reappeared, and this time they were running with all speed. Doubtless they had discovered our encampment, and had at once suspected that there were police hidden in the woods. They realized that they were watched, they were followed, they would be seized. So they dashed recklessly down the ravine, and after loosening the cable, they would doubtless endeavor to leap aboard. The Terror would disappear with the speed of a meteor, and our attempt would be wholly defeated!

"Forward," I cried. And we scrambled down the sides of the ravine to cut off the retreat of the two men.

They saw us and, on the instant, throwing down their bundles, fired at us with revolvers, hitting John Hart in the leg.

We fired in our turn, but less successfully. The men neither fell nor faltered in the course. Reaching the edge of the creek, without stopping to unloose the cable, they plunged overboard, and in a moment were clinging to the deck of the Terror.

Their captain, springing forward, revolver in hand, fired. The ball grazed Wells.

Nab Walker and I seizing the cable, pulled the black mass of the boat toward the shore. Could they cut the rope in time to escape us?

Suddenly the grappling-iron was torn violently from the rocks. One of its hooks caught in my belt, while Walker was knocked down by the flying cable. I was entangled by the iron and the rope and dragged forward—

The Terror, driven by all the power of her engines, made a single bound and darted out across Black Rock Creek.

Chapter 13

On Board the Terror

When I came to my senses it was daylight. A half light pierced the thick glass port hole of the narrow cabin wherein someone had placed me—how many hours ago, I could not say! Yet it seemed to me by the slanting rays, that the sun could not be very far above the horizon.

I was resting in a narrow bunk, with coverings over me. My clothes, hanging in a corner, had been dried. My belt, torn in half by the hook of the iron, lay on the floor.

114

I felt no wound nor injury, only a little weakness. If I had lost consciousness, I was sure it had not been from a blow. My head must have been drawn beneath the water, when I was tangled in the cable. I should have been suffocated, if someone had not dragged me from the lake.

Now, was I on board the Terror? And was I alone with the captain and his two men? This seemed probable, almost certain. The whole scene of our encounter rose before my eyes, Hart lying wounded upon the bank; Wells firing shot after shot, Walker hurled down at the instant when the grappling hook caught my belt! And my companions? On their side, must not they think that I had perished in the waters of Lake Erie?

Where was the Terror now, and how was it navigating? Was it moving as an automobile? Speeding across the roads of some neighboring state? If so, and if I had been unconscious for many hours, the machine with its tremendous powers must be already far away. Or, on the other hand, were we as a submarine, following some course beneath the lake?

No, the Terror was moving upon some broad liquid surface. The sunlight, penetrating my cabin, showed that the window was not submerged. On the other hand, I felt none of the jolting that the automobile must have suffered even on the smoothest highway. Hence the Terror was not traveling upon land.

As to deciding whether she was still traversing Lake Erie, that was another matter. Had not the captain reascended the Detroit River, and entered Lake Huron, or even Lake Superior beyond? It was difficult to say.

At any rate I decided to go up on deck. From there I might be able to judge. Dragging myself somewhat heavily from the bunk, I reached for my clothes and dressed, though without much energy. Was I not probably locked within this cabin?

The only exit seemed by a ladder and hatchway above my head. The hatch rose readily to my hand, and I ascended half way on deck.

My first care was to look forward, backward, and on both sides of the speeding Terror. Everywhere a vast expanse of waves! Not a shore in sight! Nothing but the horizon formed by sea and sky!

Whether it was a lake or the ocean I could easily settle. As we shot forward at such speed the water cut by the bow, rose furiously upward on either side, and the spray lashed savagely against me.

I tasted it. It was fresh water, and very probably that of Lake Erie. The sun was but midway toward the zenith, so it could scarcely be more than seven or eight hours since the moment when the Terror had darted from Black Rock Creek.

This must therefore be the following morning, that of the thirty-first of July.

Considering that Lake Erie is two hundred and twenty miles long and over fifty wide, there was no reason to be surprised that I could see no land, neither that of the United States to the southeast nor of Canada to the northwest.

At this moment there were two men on the deck, one being at the bow on the look-out, the other in the stern, keeping the course to the northeast, as I judged by the position of the sun. The one at the bow was he whom I had recognized as he ascended the ravine at Black Rock. The second was his companion who had carried the lantern. I looked in vain for the one whom they had called captain. He was not in sight.

It will be readily appreciated how eager was my desire to stand in the presence of the creator of this prodigious machine, of this fantastic personage who occupied and preoccupied the attention of all the world, the daring inventor who did not fear to engage in battle against the entire human race, and who proclaimed himself "Master of the World."

I approached the man on the look-out, and after a minute of silence I asked him, "Where is the captain?"

He looked at me through half-closed eyes. He seemed not to understand me. Yet I knew, having heard him the night before, that he spoke English. Moreover, I noticed that he did not appear surprised to see me out of my cabin. Turning his back upon me, he continued to search the horizon.

I stepped then toward the stern, determined to ask the same question about the captain. But when I approached the steersman, he waved me away with his hand, and I obtained no other response.

It only remained for me to study this craft,

from which we had been repelled with revolver shots, when we had seized upon its anchor rope.

I therefore set leisurely to work to examine the construction of this machine, which was carrying me—whither? The deck and the upper works were all made of some metal which I did not recognize. In the center of the deck, a scuttle half raised covered the room where the engines were working regularly and almost silently. As I had seen before, neither masts, nor rigging! Not even a flagstaff at the stern! Toward the bow there rose the top of a periscope by which the Terror could be guided when beneath the water.

On the sides were folded back two sort of outshoots resembling the gangways on certain Dutch boats. Of these I could not understand the use.

In the bow there rose a third hatchway which presumably covered the quarters occupied by the two men when the Terror was at rest.

At the stern a similar hatch gave access probably to the cabin of the captain, who remained unseen. When these different hatches were shut down, they had a sort of rubber covering which closed them hermetically tight, so that the water could not reach the interior when the boat plunged beneath the ocean.

As to the motor, which imparted such prodigious speed to the machine, I could see nothing of it, nor of the propeller. However, the fast speeding boat left behind it only a long, smooth wake. The extreme fineness of the lines of the craft, caused it to make scarcely any waves, and enabled it to ride lightly over the crest of the billows even in a rough sea.

As was already known, the power by which the machine was driven was neither steam nor gasoline, nor any of those similar liquids so well known by their odor, which are usually employed for automobiles and submarines. No doubt the power here used was electricity, generated on board, at some high power. Naturally I asked myself whence comes this electricity, from piles, or from accumulators? But how were these piles or accumulators charged? Unless, indeed, the electricity was drawn directly from the surrounding air or from the water, by processes hitherto unknown. And I asked myself with intense eagerness if in the present situation, I might be able to discover these secrets.

Then I thought of my companions, left behind on the shore of Black Rock Creek. One of them, I knew, was wounded; perhaps the others were also. Having seen me dragged overboard by the hawser, could they possibly suppose that I had been rescued by the Terror? Surely not! Doubtless the news of my death had already been telegraphed to Mr. Ward from Toledo. And now who would dare to undertake a new campaign against this "Master of the World"?

These thoughts occupied my mind as I awaited the captain's appearance on the deck. He did not appear.

I soon began to feel very hungry; for I must have fasted now nearly twenty-four hours. I had eaten nothing since our hasty meal in the woods, even if that had been the night before. And judging by the pangs which now assailed my stomach, I began to wonder if I had not been snatched on board the Terror two days before,—or even more.

Happily the question if they meant to feed me, and how they meant to feed me, was solved at once. The man at the bow left his post, descended, and reappeared. Then, without saying a word, he placed some food before me and returned to his place. Some potted meat, dried fish, sea biscuit, and a pot of ale so strong that I had to mix it with water, such was the meal to which I did full justice. My fellow travelers had doubtless eaten before I came out of the cabin, and they did not join me.

There was nothing further to attract my eyes, and I sank again into thought. How would this adventure finish? Would I see this invisible captain at length, and would he restore me to liberty? Could I regain it in spite of him? That would depend on circumstances! But if the Terror kept thus far away from the shore, or if she traveled beneath the water, how could I escape her? Unless we landed, and the machine became an automobile, must I not abandon all hope of escape?

Moreover—why should I not admit it?—to escape without having learned anything of the Terror's secrets would not have contented me at all. Although I could not thus far flatter myself upon the success of my campaign, and though I had come within a hairbreadth of losing my life, and though the future promised far more of evil than of good, yet after all, a step forward had been attained. To be sure, if I was never to be able to re-enter into communication with the world, if, like this Master of the World who had voluntarily placed himself outside the law, I was now placed outside humanity, then the fact that I had reached the Terror would have little value.

The craft continued heading to the northeast, following the longer axis of Lake Erie. She was advancing at only half speed; for had she been doing her best, she must some hours before have reached the northeastern extremity of the lake.

At this end Lake Erie has no other outlet than the Niagara River, by which it empties into Lake Ontario. Now, this river is barred by the famous cataract some fifteen miles beyond the important city of Buffalo. Since the Terror had not retreated by the Detroit River, down which she had descended from the upper lakes, how was she to escape from these waters, unless indeed she crossed by land?

The sun passed the meridian. The day was beautiful; warm but not unpleasantly so, thanks to the breeze made by our passage. The shores of the lake continued invisible, on both the Canadian and the American side.

Was the captain determined not to show himself? Had he some reason for remaining unknown? Such a precaution would indicate that he intended to set me at liberty in the evening, when the Terror could approach the shore unseen.

Toward two o'clock, however, I heard a slight noise; the central hatchway was raised. The man I had so impatiently awaited appeared on deck.

I must admit he paid no more attention to me than his men had done. Going to the stern, he took the helm. The man whom he had relieved, after a few words in a low tone, left the deck, descending by the forward hatchway. The captain, having scanned the horizon, consulted the compass, and slightly altered our course. The speed of the Terror increased.

This man, so interesting both to me and to the world, must have been some years over fifty. He was of middle height, with powerful shoulders still very erect; a strong head, with thick hair rather gray than white, smooth shaven cheeks, and a short, crisp beard. His chest was broad, his jaw prominent, and he had that characteristic sign of tremendous energy, bushy eyebrows drawn sharply together. Assuredly he possessed a constitution of iron, splendid health, and warm red blood beneath his sunburned skin.

Like his companions, the captain was dressed in sea-clothes covered by an oil-skin coat, and with a woolen cap which could be pulled down to cover his head entirely, when he so desired.

Need I add that the captain of the Terror was the other of the two men who had watched my house in Long Street. Moreover, if I recognized him, he also must recognize me as chief-inspector Strock, to whom had been assigned the task of penetrating the Great Eyrie.

I looked at him curiously. On his part, while he did not seek to avoid my eyes, he showed at least a singular indiffference to the fact that he had a stranger on board.

As I watched him, the idea came to me, a suggestion which I had not connected with the first view of him in Washington, that I had already seen this characteristic figure. Was it in one of the photographs held in the police department, or was it merely a picture in some shop window? But the remembrance was very vague. Perhaps I merely imagined it.

Well, though his companions had not had the politeness to answer me, perhaps he would be more courteous. He spoke the same language as I, although I could not feel quite positive that he was of American birth. He might indeed have decided to pretend not to understand me, so as to avoid all discussion while he held me prisoner.

In that case, what did he mean to do with me? Did he intend to dispose of me without further ceremony? Was he only waiting for night to throw me overboard? Did even the little which I knew of him make me a danger of which he must rid himself? But in that case, he might better have left me at the end of his anchor line. That would have saved him the necessity of drowning me over again.

I turned. I walked to the stern, I stopped full in front of him. Then, at length, he fixed full upon me a glance that burned like a flame.

"Are you the captain?" I asked.

He was silent.

"This boat! Is it really the Terror?"

To this question also there was no response. Then I reached toward him; I would have taken hold of his arm.

He repelled me without violence, but with a movement that suggested tremendous restrained power.

Planting myself again before him, I demanded in a louder tone, "What do you mean to do with me?"

Words seemed almost ready to burst from his lips, which he compressed with visible irritation. As though to check his speech he turned his head aside. His hand touched a regulator of some sort, and the machine rapidly increased in speed.

Anger almost mastered me. I wanted to cry out "So be it! Keep your silence! I know who you are, just as I know your machine, recognized at Madison, at Boston, at Lake Kirdall. Yes; it is you, who have rushed so recklessly over our roads, our seas and our lakes! Your boat is the Terror; and you her commander, wrote that letter to the government. It is you who fancy you can fight the entire world. You, who call yourself the Master of the World!"

And how could he have denied it! I saw at that moment the famous initials inscribed upon the helm!

Fortunately I restrained myself; and despairing of getting any response to my questions, I returned to my seat near the hatchway of my cabin.

For long hours, I patiently watched the horizon in the hope that land would soon appear. Yes, I sat waiting! For I was reduced to that! Waiting! No doubt, before the day closed, the Terror must reach the end of Lake Erie, since she continued her course steadily to the northeast.

Chapter 14

Niagara

The hours passed, and the situation did not change. The steersman returned on deck, and the captain, descending, watched the movements of the engines. Even when our speed increased, these engines continued working without noise, and with remarkable smoothness. There was never one of those inevitable breaks, with which in most motors the pistons sometimes miss a stroke. I concluded that the Terror, in each of its transformations must be worked by rotary engines. But I could not assure myself of this.

For the rest, our direction did not change. Always we headed toward the northeast end of the lake, and hence toward Buffalo.

Why, I wondered, did the captain persist in following this route? He could not intend to stop at Buffalo, in the midst of a crowd of boats and shipping of every kind. If he meant to leave the lake by water, there was only the Niagara River to follow; and its Falls would be impassable, even to such a machine as this. The only escape was by the Detroit River, and the Terror was constantly leaving that farther behind.

Then another idea occurred to me. Perhaps the captain was only waiting for night to return to the shore of the lake. There, the boat, changed to an automobile, would quickly cross the neighboring states. If I did not succeed in making my escape, during this passage across the land, all hope of regaining my liberty would be gone.

True, I might learn what no one had yet been able to discover, assuming always that he did not dispose of me at one time or another—and what I expected his "disposal" would be, is easily comprehended.

I knew the northeast end of Lake Erie well, having often visited that section of New York State which extends westward from Albany to Buffalo. Three years before, a police mission had led me to explore carefully the shores of the Niagara River, both above and below the cataract and its Suspension Bridge. I had visited the two principal islands between Buffalo and the little city of Niagara Falls; I had explored Navy Island and also Goat Island, which separates the American falls from those of the Canadian side.

Thus if an opportunity for flight presented itself, I should not find myself in an unknown district. But would this chance offer? And at heart, did I desire it, or would I seize upon it? What secrets still remained in this affair in which good fortune—or was it evil fortune—had so closely entangled me!

On the other hand, I saw no real reason to suppose that there was any chance of my reaching the shores of the Niagara River. The Terror would surely not venture into this trap which had no exit. Probably she would not even go to the extremity of the lake.

Such were the thoughts that spun through my excited brain, while my eyes remained fixed upon the empty horizon.

And always one persistent question remained insolvable. Why had the captain written to me personally that threatening letter? Why had he spied upon me in Washington? What bond attached him to the Great Eyrie? There might indeed be subterranean canals which gave him passage to Lake Kirdall, but could he pierce the impenetrable fortress of Eyrie? No! That was beyond him!

Toward four o'clock in the afternoon, reckoning by the speed of the Terror and her direction, I knew we must be approaching Buffalo; and indeed, its outlines began to show some fifteen miles ahead. During our passage, a few boats had been seen, but we had passed them at a long distance, a distance which our captain could easily keep as great as he pleased. Moreover, the Terror lay so low upon the water, that even a mile away it would have been difficult to discover her.

Now, however, the hills encircling the end of Lake Erie, came within vision, beyond Buffalo, forming the sort of funnel by which Lake Erie pour its waters into the channel of the Niagara River. Some dunes rose on the right, groups of trees stood out here and there. In the distance, several freight steamers and fishing smacks appeared. The sky became spotted with trails of smoke which were swept along by a light eastern breeze.

What was our captain thinking of in still heading toward the port of Buffalo? Did not prudence forbid him to venture further? At each moment, I expected that he would give a sweep of the helm and turn away toward the western shore of the lake. Or else, I thought, he would prepare to plunge beneath the surface. But this persistence in holding our bow toward Buffalo was impossible to understand!

At length the helmsman, whose eyes were watching the northeastern shore, made a sign to his companion. The latter, leaving the bow, went to the central hatchway, and descended into the engine room. Almost immediately the captain came on deck, and joining the helmsman, spoke with him in a low voice.

The latter, extending his hand toward Buffalo, pointed out two black spots, which showed five or six miles distant on the starboard side. The captain studied them attentively. Then shrugging his shoulders, he seated himself at the stern without altering the course of the Terror.

A quarter of an hour later, I could see plainly that there were two smoke clouds at the point they had studied so carefully. Little by little the black spots beneath these became more defined.

They were two long, low steamers, which, coming from the port of Buffalo, were approaching rapidly.

Suddenly it struck me that these were the two torpedo destroyers of which Mr. Ward had spoken, and which I had been told to summon in case of need.

These destroyers were of the newest type, the swiftest boats yet constructed in the country. Driven by powerful engines of the latest make, they had covered almost thirty miles an hour. It is true, the Terror commanded an even greater speed, and always, if she were surrounded so that flight was impossible, she could submerge herself out of reach of all pursuit. In truth, the destroyers would have had to be submarines to attack the Terror with any chance of success. And I knew not, if even in that case, the contest would have been equal.

Meanwhile, it seemed to me evident that the commanders of the two ships had been warned, perhaps by Mr. Wells who, returning swiftly to Toledo, might have telegraphed to them the news of our defeat. It appeared, moreover, that they had seen the Terror, for they were headed at full speed toward her. Yet our captain, seemingly giving them no thought whatever, continued his course toward the Niagara River.

What would the torpedo destroyers do? Presumably, they would maneuver so as to shut the Terror within the narrowing end of the lake where the Niagara offered her no passage.

Our captain now took the helm. One of the men was at the bow, the other in the engine room.

Would the order be given for me to go down into the cabin?

It was not, to my extreme satisfaction. To speak frankly, no one paid any attention to me. It was as if I had not been on board. I watched, therefore, not without mixed emotions, the approach of the destroyers. Less than two miles distant now they separated in such a way as to hold the Terror between their fires.

As to the Master of the World, his manner indicated only the most profound disdain. He seemed sure that these destroyers were powerless against him. With a touch of his machinery he could distance them, no matter what their speed! With a few turns of her engine, the Terror would dart beyond their cannon shots! Or, in the depths of the lake, what projectiles could find the submarine?

Five minutes later, scarcely a mile separated us from the two powerful fighters which pursued us. Our captain permitted them to approach still closer. Then he pressed upon a handle. The Terror, doubling the action of her propellers, leaped across the surface of the lake. She played with the destroyers! Instead of turning in flight, she continued her forward course. Who knew if she would not even have the audacity to pass between her two enemies, to coax them after her, until the hour when, as night closed in, they would be forced to abandon the useless pursuit!

The city of Buffalo was now in plain view on the border of the lake. I saw its huge buildings, its church towers, its grain elevators. Only four or five miles ahead, Niagara River opened to the northward.

Under these new conditions which way should I turn? When we passed in front of the destroyers, or perhaps between them, should I throw myself into the water? I was a good swimmer, and such a chance might never occur again. The captain could not stop to recapture me. By diving could I not easily escape, even from a bullet? I should surely be seen by one or other of the pursuers. Perhaps, even, their commanders had been warned of my presence on board the Terror. Would not a boat be sent to rescue me?

Evidently my chance of success would be even greater, if the Terror entered the narrow waters of Niagara River. At Navy Island I would be able to set foot on territory that I knew well. But to suppose that our captain would rush into this river where he might be swept over the great cataract! That seemed impossible! I resolved to await the destroyer's closest approach and at the last moment I would decide.

Yet my resolution to escape was but half-hearted. I could not resign myself thus to lose all chance of following up this mystery. My instincts as a police official revolted. I had but to reach out my hand in order to seize this man who had been outlawed! Should I let him escape me? No! I would not save myself! Yet, on the other hand, what fate awaited me, and where would I be carried by the Terror, if I remained on board?

It was a quarter past six. The destroyers, quivering and trembling under the strain of their speed, gained on us perceptibly. They were now directly astern, leaving between them a distance of twelve or fifteen cable lengths. The Terror, without increasing her speed, saw one of them approach on the port side, the other to the starboard.

I did not leave my place. The man at the bow was close by me. Immovable at the helm, his eyes burning beneath his contracted brows, the captain waited. He meant, perhaps, to finish the chase by one last maneuver.

Suddenly, a puff of smoke rose from the destroyer on our left. A projectile, brushing the surface of the water, passed in front of the Terror, and sped beyond the destroyer on our right.

I glanced around anxiously. Standing by my side, the lookout seemed to await a sign from the captain. As for him, he did not even turn his head; and I shall never forget the expression of disdain imprinted on his visage.

At this moment, I was pushed suddenly toward the hatchway of my cabin, which was fastened above me. At the same instant the other hatchways were closed; the deck became watertight. I heard a single throb of the machinery, and the plunge was made, the submarine disappeared beneath the waters of the lake.

Cannon shot still boomed above us. Their heavy echo reached my ear; then everything was peace. Only a faint light penetrated through the porthole in my cabin. The submarine, without the least rolling or pitching, sped silently through the deeps.

I had seen with what rapidity, and also with what ease the transformation of the Terror had been made. No less easy and rapid, perhaps, would be her change to an automobile.

And now what would this Master of the World do? Presumably he would change his course, unless, indeed, he preferred to speed to land, and there continue his route along the roads. It still seemed more probable, however, that he would turn back toward the west, and after distancing the destroyers, regain the Detroit River. Our submersion would probably only last long enough to escape out of cannon range, or until night forbade pursuit.

Fate, however, had decreed a different ending to this exciting chase. Scarce ten minutes had passed when there seemed some confusion on board. I heard rapid words exchanged in the engine room. The steadily moving machinery became noisy and irregular. At once I suspected that some accident compelled the submarine to reascend.

I was not mistaken. In a moment, the semi-obscurity of my cabin was pierced by sunshine. The Terror had risen above water. I heard steps on deck, and the hatchways were re-opened, including mine. I sprang up the ladder.

The captain had resumed his place at the helm, while the two men were busy below. I looked to see if the destroyers were still in view. Yes! Only a quarter of a mile away! The Terror had already been seen, and the powerful vessels which enforced the mandates of our government were swinging into position to give chase. Once more the Terror sped in the direction of Niagara River.

I must confess, I could make nothing of this maneuver. Plunging into a cul-de-sac, no longer able to seek the depths because of the accident,

the Terror might, indeed, temporarily distance
her pursuers; but she must find her path barred
by them when she attempted to return. Did she
intend to land, and if so, could she hope to outrun
the telegrams which would warn every police
agency of her approach?

We were now not half a mile ahead. The
destroyers pursued us at top speed, though being
now directly behind, they were in poor position
for using their guns. Our captain seemed content
to keep his distance; though it would have been
easy for him to increase it, and then at nightfall,
to dodge back behind the enemy.

Already Buffalo had disappeared on our right,
and a litle after seven o'clock the opening of the
Niagara River appeared ahead. If he entered
there, knowing that he could not return, our
captain must have lost his mind! And in truth was
he not insane, this man who proclaimed himself,
who believed himself, Master of the World?

I watched him there, calm, impassive not even
turning his head to note the progress of the
destroyers and I wondered at him.

This end of the lake was absolutely deserted.
Freight steamers bound for the towns on the
banks of the upper Niagara are not numerous, as
its navigation is dangerous. Not one was in sight.
Not even a fishing-boat crossed the path of the
Terror. Even the two destroyers would soon be
obliged to pause in their pursuit, if we continued
our mad rush through these dangerous waters.

I have said that the Niagara River flows between New York and Canada. Its width, of about
three quarters of a mile, narrows as it approaches

the falls. Its length, from Lake Erie to Lake Ontario, is about fifteen leagues. It flows in a northerly direction, until it empties the waters of Lake Superior, Michigan, Huron, and Erie, into Ontario, the west lake of this mighty chain. The celebrated falls, which occur in the midst of this great river have a height of over a hundred and fifty feet. They are called sometimes the Horseshoe Falls, because they curve inward like the iron shoe. The Indians have given them the name of "Thunder of Waters," and in truth a mighty thunder roars from them without cessation, and with a tumult which is heard for several miles away.

Between Lake Erie, and the little city of Niagara Falls, two islands divide the current of the river, Navy Island, a league above the cataract, and Goat Island, which separates the American and the Canadian Falls. Indeed, on the lower point of this latter isle stood once that "Terrapin Tower" so daringly built in the midst of the plunging waters on the very edge of the abyss. It has been destroyed; for the constant wearing away of the stone beneath the cataract makes the ledge move with the ages slowly up the river, and the tower has been drawn into the gulf.

The town of Fort Erie stands on the Canadian shore at the entrance of the river. Two other towns are set along the banks above the falls, Schlosser on the right bank, and Chippewa on the left, located on either side of Navy Island. It is at this point that the current, bound within a narrower channel, begins to move at tremendous speed, to become two miles further on, the celebrated cataract.

The Terror had already passed Fort Erie. The sun in the west touched the edge of the Canadian horizon, and the moon faintly seen, rose above the mists of the south. Darkness would not envelop us for another hour.

The destroyers, with huge clouds of smoke streaming from their funnels, followed us a mile behind. They sped between banks green with shade trees and dotted with cottages which lay among lovely gardens.

Obviously the Terror could no longer turn back. The destroyers shut her in completely. It is true their commanders did not know, as I did, that an accident to her machinery had forced her to surface, and that it ws impossible for her to escape them by another plunge. Nevertheless, they continued to follow, assuredly maintaining their pursuit to the very last.

I marveled at the intrepidity of their chase through these dangerous waters. I marveled still more at the conduct of our captain. Within a half hour now, his course would be barred by the cataract. No matter how perfect his machine, it could not escape the power of the great falls. If the current once mastered our engines, we should inevitably disappear in the gulf nearly two hundred feet deep which the waters have dug at the base of the falls! Perhaps, however, our captain still had power to turn to one of the shores and flee by the automobile routes.

In the midst of this excitement, what action should I take personally? Should I attempt to gain the shores of Navy Island, if we indeed advanced that far? If I did not seize this chance, never after what I had learned of his secrets, never would the Master of the World restore me to liberty.

I suspected, however, that my flight was no longer possible. If I was not confined within my cabin, I no longer remained unwatched. While the captain retained his place at the helm, his assistant by my side never removed his eyes from me. At the first movement, I should be seized and locked within my room. For the present, my fate was evidently bound up with that of the Terror.

The distance which separated us from the two destroyers was now growing rapidly less. Soon they were but a few cable lengths away. Could the motor of the Terror, since the accident, no longer hold its speed? Yet the captain showed not the least anxiety, and made no effort to reach land!

We could hear the hissing of the steam which escaped from the valves of the destroyers to mingle with the streamers of black smoke. But we heard, even more plainly, the roar of the cataract, now less than three miles away.

The Terror took the left branch of the river in passing Navy Island. At this point, she was within easy reach of the shore, yet she shot ahead. Five minutes later, we could see the first trees of Goat Island. The current became more and more irresistible. If the Terror did not stop, the destroyers could not much longer follow her. If it pleased our accursed captain to plunge us into the vortex of the falls, surely they did not mean to follow into the abyss!

Indeed, at this moment they signaled each other, and stopped the pursuit. They were scarce more than six hundred feet from the cataract.

Then their thunders burst on the air and several cannon shot swept over the Terror without hitting its low-lying deck.

The sun had set, and through the twilight the moon's rays shone upon us from the south. The speed of our craft, doubled by the speed of the current, was prodigious! In another moment, we should plunge into that black hollow which forms the very center of the Canadian Falls.

With an eye of horror, I saw the shores of Goat Island flash by, then came the Isles of the Three Sisters, drowned in the spray from the abyss.

I sprang up; I started to throw myself into the water, in the desperate hope of gaining this last refuge. One of the men seized me from behind.

Suddenly a sharp noise was heard from the mechanism which throbbed within our craft. The long gangways folded back on the sides of the machine, spread out like wings, and at the moment when the Terror reached the very edge of the falls, she arose into space, escaping from the thundering cataract in the center of a lunar rainbow.

Chapter 15

The Eagle's Nest

On the morrow, when I awoke after a sound sleep, our vehicle seemed motionless. It seemed to me evident that we were not running upon land. Yet neither were we rushing through or beneath the waters; nor yet soaring across the sky. Had the inventor regained that mysterious hiding place of his, where no human being had ever set foot before him?

And now since he had not disembarrassed himself of my presence, was his secret about to be revealed to me?

It seemed astonishing that I had slept so profoundly during most of our voyage through the air. It puzzled me and I asked if this sleep had not been caused by some drug, mixed with my last meal, the captain of the Terror having wished thus to prevent me from knowing the place where we landed. All that I can recall of the previous night is the terrible impression made upon me by that moment when the machine, instead of being caught in the vortex of the cataract rose under the impulse of its machinery like a bird with its huge wings beating with tremendous power!

So this machine actually fulfilled a four-fold use! It was at the same time automobile, boat, submarine, and airship. Earth, sea and air—it could move through all three elements! And with what power! With what speed! A few instants sufficed to complete its marvelous transformations. The same engine drove it along all its courses! And I had been a witness of its metamorphoses! But that of which I was still ignorant, and which I could perhaps discover, was the source of the energy which drove the machine, and above all, who was the inspired inventor who, after having created it, in every detail, guided it with so much ability and audacity!

At the moment when the Terror rose above the Canadian Falls, I was held down against the hatchway of my cabin. The clear, moonlit evening had permitted me to note the direction taken by the airship. It followed the course of the river and passed the Suspension Bridge three miles below the falls. It is here that the irresistible rapids of the Niagara River begin, where the river bends sharply to descend toward Lake Ontario.

On leaving this point, I was sure that we had turned toward the east. The captain continued at the helm. I had not addressed a word to him. What good would it do? He would not have answered. I noted that the Terror seemed to be guided in its course through the air with surprising ease. Assuredly the roads of the air were as familiar to it as those of the seas and of the lands!

In the presence of such results, could one not understand the enormous pride of this man who proclaimed himself Master of the World? Was he not in control of a machine infinitely superior to any that had ever sprung from the hand of man, and against which men were powerless? In truth, why should he sell this marvel? Why should he accept the millions offered him? Yes, I comprehended now that absolute confidence in himself which was expressed in his every attitude. And where might not his ambition carry him, if by its own excess it mounted some day into madness!

A half hour after the Terror soared into the air, I had sunk into complete unconsciousness, without realizing its approach. I repeat, it must have been caused by some drug. Without doubt, our commander did not wish me to know the road he followed.

Hence I cannot say whether the aviator continued his flight through space, or whether the mariner sailed the surface of some sea or lake, or the chauffeur sped across the American roads. No recollection remains with me of what passed during that night of July thirty-first.

Now, what was to follow from this adventure? And especially concerning myself, what would be its end?

I have said that at the moment when I awoke from my strange sleep, the Terror seemed to me completely motionless. I could hardly be mistaken; whatever had been her method of progress, I should have felt some movement, even in the air. I lay in my berth in the cabin, where I had been shut in without knowing it, just as I had been on the preceding night which I had passed on board the Terror on Lake Erie.

My business now was to learn if I would be allowed to go on deck here where the machine had landed. I attempted to raise the hatchway. It was fastened.

"Ah!" said I. "Am I to be kept here until the Terror recommences its travels?" Was not that indeed, the only time when escape was hopeless?

My impatience and anxiety may be appreciated. I knew not how long this halt might continue.

I had not a quarter of an hour to wait. A noise of bars being removed came to my ear. The hatchway was raised from above. A wave of light and air penetrated my cabin.

With one bound I reached the deck. My eyes in an instant swept round the horizon.

The Terror, as I had thought, rested quiet on the ground. She was in the midst of a rocky hollow measuring from fifteen to eighteen hundred feet in circumference. A floor of yellow gravel carpeted its entire extent, unrelieved by a single tuft of herbage.

This hollow formed an almost regular oval, with its longer diameter extending north and south. As to the surrounding wall, what was its height, what the character of its crest, I could not judge. Above us was gathered a fog so heavy, that the rays of the sun had not yet pierced it. Heavy trails of cloud drifted across the sandy floor. Doubtless the morning was still young, and this mist might later be dissolved.

It was quite cold here, although this was the first day of August. I concluded therefore that he must be far in the north, or else high above sea level. We must still be somewhere on the New Continent; though where, it was impossible to surmise. Yet no matter how rapid our flight had been, the airship could not have traversed either ocean in the dozen hours since our departure from Niagara.

At this moment, I saw the captain come from an opening in the rocks, probably a grotto, at the base of this cliff hidden in the fog. Occasionally, in the mists above, appeared the shadows of huge birds. Their raucous cries were the sole interruption to the profound silence. Who knows if they were not frightened by the arrival of this formidable, winged monster, which they could not match either in might or speed.

Everything led me to believe that it was here that the Master of the World withdrew in the intervals between his prodigious journeys. Here was the garage of his automobile; the harbor of his boat; the hangar of his airship.

And now the Terror stood motionless at the bottom of this hollow. At last I could examine her; and it looked as if her owners had no intention of preventing me. The truth is that the commander seemed to take no more notice of my presence than before. His two companions joined him, and the three did not hesitate to enter together into the grotto I had seen. What a chance to study the machine, at least its exterior! As to its inner parts, probably I should never get beyond conjecture.

In fact, except for that of my cabin, the hatchways were closed; and it would be vain for me to attempt to open them. At any rate, it might be more interesting to find out what kind of propeller drove the Terror in these many transformations.

I jumped to the ground and found I was left at leisure, to proceed with this first examination.

The machine was as I have said spindle-shaped. The bow was sharper than the stern. The body was of aluminum, the wings of a substance whose nature I could not determine. The body rested on four wheels, about two feet in diameter. These had pneumatic tires so thick as to assure ease of movement at any speed. Their spokes spread out like paddles or battledores; and when the Terror moved either on or under the water, they must have increased her pace.

These wheels were not, however, the principal propeller. This consisted of two "Parsons" turbines placed on either side of the keel. Driven with extreme rapidity by the engine, they urged the boat onward in the water by twin screws, and I even questioned if they were not powerful enough to propel the machine through the air.

The chief aerial support, however, was that of the great wings, now again in repose, and folded back along the sides. Thus the theory of the "heavier than air" flying machine was employed by the inventor, a system which enabled him to dart through space with a speed probably superior to that of the largest birds.

As to the agent which set in action these various mechanisms, I repeat, it was, it could be, no other than electricity. But from what source did his batteries get their power? Had he somewhere an electric factory, to which he must return? Were the dynamos, perhaps working in one of the caverns of this hollow?

The result of my examination was that, while I could see that the machine used wheels and turbine screws and wings, I knew nothing of either its engine, nor of the force which drove it. To be sure, the discovery of this secret would be of little value to me. To employ it I must first be free. And after what I knew—little as that really was—the Master of the World would never release me.

There remained, it is true, the chance of escape. But would an opportunity ever present itself? If there could be none during the voyages of the Terror, might there possibly be, while we remained in this retreat?

The first question to be solved was the location of this hollow. What communication did it have with the surrounding region? Could one only depart from it by a flying-machine? And in what part of the United States were we? Was it not reasonable to estimate, that our flight through the darkness had covered several hundred leagues?

There was one very natural hypothesis which deserved to be considered, if not actually accepted. What more natural harbor could there be for the Terror than the Great Eyrie? Was it too difficult a flight for our aviator to reach the summit? Could he not soar anywhere that the vultures and the eagles could? Did not that inaccessible Eyrie offer to the Master of the World just such a retreat as our police had been unable to discover, one in which he might well believe himself safe from all attacks? Moreover, the distance between Niagara Falls and this part of the Blue Ridge Mountains, did not exceed four hundred and fifty miles, a flight which would have been easy for the Terror.

Yes, this idea more and more took possession of me. It crowded out a hundred other unsupported suggestions. Did not this explain the nature of the bond which existed between the Great Eyrie and the letter which I had received with our commander's initials? And the threats against me if I renewed the ascent! And the espionage to which I had been subjected! And all the phenomena of which the Great Eyrie had been the theater, were they not to be attributed to this same cause—though what lay behind the phenomena was not yet clear? Yes, the Great Eyrie! The Great Eyrie!

But since it had been impossible for me to penetrate here, would it not be equally impossible for me to get out again, except upon the Terror? Ah, if the mists would but lift! Perhaps I should recognize the place. What was as yet a mere hypothesis, would become a starting point to act upon.

However, since I had freedom to move about, since neither the captain nor his men paid any heed to me, I resolved to explore the hollow. The three of them were all in the grotto toward the north end of the oval. Therefore I would commence my inspection at the southern end.

Reaching the rocky wall, I skirted along its base and found it broken by many crevices; above, arose more solid rocks of that feldspar of which the chain of the Alleghenies largely consists. To what height the rock wall rose, or what was the character of its summit, was still impossible to see. I must wait until the sun had scattered the mists.

In the meantime, I continued to follow along the base of the cliff. None of its cavities seemed to extend inward to any distance. Several of them contained debris from the hand of man, bits of broken wood, heaps of dried grasses. On the ground were still to be seen the footprints that the captain and his men must have left, perhaps months before, upon the sand.

My jailers, being doubtless very busy in their cabin, did not show themselves until they had arranged and packed several large bundles. Did they purpose to carry those on board the Terror? And were they packing up with the intention of permanently leaving their retreat?

In half an hour my explorations were completed and I returned toward the center. Here and there were heaped up piles of ashes, bleached by weather. There were fragments of burned planks and beams; posts to which clung rusted iron-work; armatures of metal twisted by fire; all the remnants of some intricate mechanism destroyed by the flames.

Clearly at some period not very remote the hollow had been the scene of a conflagration, accidental or intentional. Naturally I connected this with the phenomena observed at the Great

Eyrie, the flames which rose above the crest, the noises which had so frightened the people of Pleasant Garden and Morganton. But of what mechanisms were these the fragments, and what reason had our captain for destroying them?

At this moment I felt a breath of air; a breeze came from the east. The sky swiftly cleared. The hollow was filled with light from the rays of the sun which appeared midway between the horizon and the zenith.

A cry escaped me! The crest of the rocky wall rose a hundred feet above me. And on the eastern side was revealed that easily recognizable pinnacle, the rock like a mounting eagle. It was the same that had held the attention of Mr. Elias Smith and myself, when we had looked up at it from the outer side of the Great Eyrie.

Thus there was no further doubt. In its flight during the night the airship had covered the distance between Lake Erie and North Carolina. It was in the depth of this Eyrie that the machine had found shelter! This was the nest, worthy of the gigantic and powerful bird created by the genius of our captain! The fortress whose mighty walls none but he could scale! Perhaps even, he had discovered in the depths of some cavern some subterranean passage by which he himself could quit the Great Eyrie, leaving the Terror safely sheltered within.

At last I saw it all! This explained the first letter sent me from the Great Eyrie itself with the threat of death. If we had been able to penetrate into this hollow, who knows if the secrets of the Master of the World might not have been discovered before he had been able to set them beyond our reach?

I stood there, motionless; my eyes fixed on that mounting eagle of stone, prey to a sudden, violent emotion. Whatsoever might be the consequences to myself, was it not my duty to destroy this machine, here and now, before it could resume its menacing flight of mastery across the world!

Steps approached behind me. I turned. The inventor stood by my side, and pausing looked me in the face.

I was unable to restrain myself; the words burst forth—"The Great Eyrie! The Great Eyrie!"

"Yes, Inspector Strock."

"And you! You are the Master of the World?"

"Of that world to which I have already proved myself to be the most powerful of men."

"You!" I reiterated, stupefied with amazement.

"I," responded he, drawing himself up in all his pride, "I, Robur—Robur, the Conqueror!"

Chapter 16

Robur, the Conqueror

Robur, the Conqueror! This then was the likeness I had vaguely recalled. Some years before the portrait of this extraordinary man had been printed in all the American newspapers, under date of the thirteenth of June, the day after this personage had made his sensational appearance at the meeting of the Weldon Institute at Philadelphia.

I had noted the striking character of the portrait at the time; the square shoulders; the back like a regular trapezoid, its longer side formed by that geometrical shoulder line; the robust neck; the enormous spheroidal head. The eyes at the least emotion burned with fire, while above them were the heavy, permanently contracted brows, which signalized such energy. The hair was short and crisp, with a glitter of metal in its light. The huge breast rose and fell like a blacksmith's forge; and the thighs, the arms and hands, were worthy of the mighty body. The narrow head was the same also, with the smooth shaven cheeks which showed the powerful muscles of the jaw.

And this was Robur the Conqueror, who now stood before me, who revealed himself to me, hurling forth his name like a threat, within his own impenetrable fortress!

Let me recall briefly the facts which had previously drawn upon Robur the Conqueror the attention of the entire world. The Weldon Institute was a club devoted to aeronautics under the presidency of one of the chief personages of Philadelphia commonly called Uncle Prudent. Its secretary was Mr. Phillip Evans. The members of the Institute were devoted to the theory of the "lighter than air" machine; and under their two leaders were constructing an enormous dirigible balloon, the Goahead.

At a meeting in which they were discussing the details of the construction of their balloon, this unknown Robur had suddenly appeared and, ridiculing all their plans, had insisted that the only true solution of flight lay with the heavier than air machines, and that he had proven this by constructing one.

He was in his turn doubted and ridiculed by the members of the club, who called him in mockery Robur the Conqueror. In the tumult that followed, revolver shots were fired; and the intruder disappeared.

That same night he had by force abducted the president and the secretary of the club, and had taken them, much against their will, upon a voyage in the wonderful airship the Albatross which he had constructed. He meant thus to prove to them beyond argument the correctness of his assertions. This ship, a hundred feet long, was upheld in the air by a large number of horizontal screws and was driven forward by vertical screws at its bow and stern. It was managed by a crew of at least half a dozen men, who seemed absolutely devoted to their leader, Robur.

After a voyage almost completely around the world, Mr. Prudent and Mr. Evans managed to escape from the Albatross after a desperate struggle. They even managed to cause an explosion on the airship, destroying it, and involving the inventor and all his crew in a terrific fall from the sky into the Pacific Ocean.

Mr. Prudent and Mr. Evans then returned to Philadelphia. They had learned that the Albatross had been constructed on an unknown isle of the Pacific called Island X; but since the location of this hiding place was wholly unknown, its discovery lay scarcely within the bounds of possibility. Moreover, the search seemed entirely unnecessary, as the vengeful prisoners were quite certain that they had destroyed their jailers.

Hence the two millionaires, restored to their homes, went calmly on with the construction of their own machine, the Goahead. They hoped by means of it to soar once more into the regions they had traversed with Robur, and to prove to themselves that their lighter than air machine was at least the equal of the heavy Albatross. If they had not persisted, they would not have been true Americans.

On the twentieth of April in the following year the Goahead was finished and the ascent was made, from Fairmount Park in Philadelphia. I myself was there with thousands of other spectators. We saw the huge balloon rise gracefully; and, thanks to its powerful screws, it maneuvered in every direction with surprising ease. Suddenly a cry was heard, a cry repeated from a thousand throats. Another airship had appeared in the distant skies and it now approached with marvelous rapidity. It was another Albatross, perhaps even superior to the first. Robur and his men had escaped death in the Pacific; and, burning for revenge, they had constructed a second airship in their secret Island X.

Like a gigantic bird of prey, the Albatross hurled itself upon the Goahead. Doubtless, Robur, while avenging himself wished also to prove the immeasurable superiority of the heavier than air machines.

Mr. Prudent and Mr. Evans defended themselves as best they could. Knowing that their balloon had nothing like the horizontal speed of the Albatross, they attempted to take advantage of their superior lightness and rise above her. The Goahead, throwing out all her ballast, soared to a height of over twenty thousand feet. Yet even there the Albatross rose above her, and circled round her with ease.

Suddenly an explosion was heard. The enormous gas-bag of the Goahead, expanding under the dilation of its contents at this great height, had finally burst.

Half-emptied, the balloon fell rapidly.

Then, to our universal astonishment, the Albatross shot down after her rival, not to finish the work of destruction but to bring rescue. Yes! Robur, forgetting his vengeance, rejoined the sinking Goahead, and his men lifted Mr. Prudent, Mr. Evans, and the aeronaut who accompanied them, onto the platform of his craft. Then the balloon, being at length entirely empty, fell to its destruction among the trees of Fairmount Park.

The public was overwhelmed with astonishment, with fear! Now that Robur had recaptured his prisoners, how would he avenge himself? Would they be carried away, this time, forever?

The Albatross continued to descend, as if to land in the clearing at Fairmount Park. But if it came within reach, would not the infuriated crowd throw themselves upon the airship, tearing both it and its inventor to pieces?

The Albatross descended within six feet of the ground. I remember well the general movement forward with which the crowd threatened to attack it. Then Robur's voice rang out in words which even now I can repeat almost as he said them:

"Citizens of the United States, the president and the secretary of the Weldon Institute are again in my power. In holding them prisoners I would but be exercising my natural right of reprisal for the injuries they have done me. But the passion and resentment which have been roused both in them and you by the success of the Albatross, show that the souls of men are not yet ready for the vast increase of power which the conquest of the air will bring to them. Uncle Prudent, Phillip Evans, you are free."

The three men rescued from the balloon leaped to the ground. The airship rose some thirty feet out of reach, and Robur recommenced:

"Citizens of the United States, the conquest of the air is made; but it shall not be given into your hands until the proper time. I leave, and I carry my secret with me. It will not be lost to humanity, but shall be entrusted to them when they have learned not to abuse it. Farewell, citizens of the United States!"

Then the Albatross rose under the impulse of its mighty screws, and sped away amidst the hurrahs of the multitude.

I have ventured to remind my readers of this last scene somewhat in detail, because it seemed to reveal the state of mind of the remarkable personage who now stood before me. Apparently he had not then been animated by sentiments hostile to humanity. He was content to await the future; though his attitude undeniably revealed the immeasurable confidence which he had in his own genius, the immense pride which his almost superhuman powers had aroused within him.

It was not astonishing, moreover, that this haughtiness had little by little been aggravated to such a degree that he now presumed to enslave the entire world, as his public letter had suggested by its significant threats. His vehement mind had with time been roused to such over-excitement that he might easily be driven into the most violent excesses.

As to what had happened in the years since the last departure of the Albatross, I could only partly reconstruct this even with my present knowledge.

It had not sufficed the prodigious inventor to create a flying machine, perfect as that was! He had planned to construct a machine which could conquer all the elements at once. Probably in the workshops of Island X, a selected body of devoted workmen had constructed, one by one, the pieces of this marvelous machine, with its quadruple transformation. Then the second Albatross must have carried these pieces to the Great Eyrie, where they had been put together, within easier access of the world of men than the far-off island had permitted. The Albatross itself had apparently been destroyed, whether by accident or design, within the Eyrie. The Terror had then made its appearance on the roads of the United States and in the neighboring waters. And I have told under what conditions, after having been vainly pursued across Lake Erie, this remarkable masterpiece had risen through the air carrying me a prisoner on board.

Chapter 17

In the Name of the Law

What was to be the issue of this remarkable adventure? Could I bring it to any dénouement whatever, either sooner or later? Did not Robur hold the results wholly in his own hands? Probably I would never have such an opportunity for escape as had occurred to Mr. Prudent and Mr. Evans amid the islands of the Pacific. I could only wait. And how long might the waiting last!

To be sure, my curiosity had been partly satisfied. But even now I knew only the answer to the problems of the Great Eyrie. Having at length penetrated its circle, I comprehended all the phenomena observed by the people of the Blue Ridge Mountains. I was assured that neither the countryfolk throughout the region, nor the townfolk of Pleasant Garden and Morganton were in danger of volcanic eruptions or earthquakes. No subterranean forces whatever were battling within the bowels of the mountains. No crater had arisen in this corner of the Alleghenies. The Great Eyrie served merely as the retreat of Robur the Conqueror. This impenetrable hiding place where he stored his materials and provisions, had without doubt been discovered by him during one of his aerial voyages in the Albatross. It was a retreat probably even more secure than that as yet undiscovered Island X in the Pacific.

This much I knew of him; but of this marvelous machine of his, of the secrets of its construction and propelling force, what did I really know? Admitting that this multiple mechanism was driven by electricity, and that this electricity was, as we knew it had been in the Albatross, extracted directly from the surrounding air by some new process, what were the details of its mechanism? I had not been permitted to see the engine; doubtless I should never see it.

On the question of my liberty I argued thus: Robur evidently intends to remain unknown. As to what he intends to do with his machine, I fear, recalling his letter, that the world must expect from it more of evil than of good. At any rate, the incognito which he has so carefully guarded in the past he must mean to preserve in the future. Now only one man can establish the identity of the Master of the World with Robur the Conqueror. This man is I his prisoner, I who have the right to arrest him, I, who ought to put my hand on his shoulder, saying, "In the Name of the Law—"

On the other hand, could I hope for a rescue from without? Evidently not. The police authorities must know everything that had happened at Black Rock Creek. Mr. Ward, advised of all the incidents, would have reasoned on the matter as follows: when the Terror quitted the creek dragging me at the end of her hawser, I had either been drowned or, since my body had not been recovered, I had been taken on board the Terror, and was in the hands of its commander.

In the first case, there was nothing more to do than to write "deceased" after the name of John Strock, chief inspector of the federal police in Washington.

In the second case, could my confreres hope ever to see me again? The two destroyers which had pursued the Terror into the Niagara River had stopped, perforce, when the current threatened to drag them over the falls. At that moment, night was closing in, and what could be thought on board the destroyers but that the Terror had been engulfed in the abyss of the cataract? It was scarce possible that our machine had been seen when, amid the shades of night, it rose above the Horseshoe Falls, or when it winged its way high above the mountains on its route to the Great Eyrie.

With regard to my own fate, should I resolve to

question Robur? Would he consent even to appear to hear me? Was he not content with having hurled at me his name? Would not that name seem to him to answer everything?

That day wore away without bringing the least change to the situation. Robur and his men continued actively at work upon the machine, which apparently needed considerable repair. I concluded that they meant to start forth again very shortly, and to take me with them. It would, however, have been quite possible to leave me at the bottom of the Eyrie. There would have been no way by which I could have escaped, and there were provisions at hand sufficient to keep me alive for many days.

What I studied particularly during this period was the mental state of Robur. He seemed to me under the dominance of a continuous excitement. What was it that his ever-seething brain now meditated? What projects was he forming for the future? Toward what region would he now turn? Would he put in execution the menaces expressed in his letter—the menaces of a madman!

The night of that first day, I slept on a couch of dry grass in one of the grottoes of the Great Eyrie. Food was set for me in this grotto each succeeding day. On the second and third of August, the three men continued at their work, scarcely once, however, exchanging any words, even in the midst of their labors. When the engines were all repaired to Robur's satisfaction, the men began putting stores aboard their craft, as if expecting a long absence. Perhaps the Terror was about to traverse immense distances; perhaps even, the captain intended to regain his Island X, in the midst of the Pacific.

Sometimes I saw him wander about the eyrie buried in thought, or he would stop and raise his arm toward heaven as if in defiance of that God with Whom he assumed to divide the empire of the world. Was not his overweening pride leading him toward insanity? An insanity which his two companions, hardly less excited than he, could do nothing to subdue! Had he not come to regard himself as mightier than the elements which he had so audaciously defied even when he possessed only an airship, the Albatross? And now, how much more powerful had he become, when earth, air and water combined to offer him an infinite field where none might follow him!

Hence I had much to fear from the future, even the most dread catastrophes. It was impossible for me to escape from the Great Eyrie, before being dragged into a new voyage. After that, how could I possibly get away while the Terror sped through the air or the ocean? My only chance must be when she crossed the land, and did so at some moderate speed. Surely a distant and feeble hope to cling to!

It will be recalled that after our arrival at the Great Eyrie, I had attempted to obtain some response from Robur, as to his purpose with me; but I had failed. On this last day I made another attempt.

In the afternoon I walked up and down before the large grotto where my captors were at work. Robur, standing at the entrance, followed me steadily with his eyes. Did he mean to address me?

I went up to him. "Captain," said I, "I have already asked you a question, which you have not answered. I ask it again: What do you intend to do with me?"

We stood face to face scarce two steps apart. With arms folded, he glared at me, and I was terrified by his glance. Terrified, that is the word! The glance was not that of a sane man. Indeed, it seemed to reflect nothing whatever of humanity within.

I repeated my question in a more challenging tone. For an instant I thought that Robur would break his silence and burst forth.

"What do you intend to do with me? Will you set me free?"

Evidently my captor's mind was obsessed by some other thought, from which I had only distracted him for a moment. He made again that gesture which I had already observed; he raised one defiant arm toward the zenith. It seemed to me as if some irresistible force drew him toward those upper zones of the sky, that he belonged no more to the earth, that he was destined to live in space, a perpetual dweller in the clouds.

Without answering me, without seeming to have understood me, Robur re-entered the grotto.

How long this sojourn or rather relaxation of the Terror in the Great Eyrie was to last, I did not know. I saw, however, on the afternoon of this third of August that the repairs and the embarkation of stores were completed. The hold and lockers of our craft must have been completely crowded with the provisions taken from the grottoes of the Eyrie.

Then the chief of the two assistants, a man whom I now recognized as that John Turner who had been mate of the Albatross, began another labor. With the help of his companion, he dragged to the center of the hollow all that remained of their materials, empty cases, fragments of carpentry, peculiar pieces of wood which clearly must have belonged to the Albatross, which had been sacrificed to this new and mightier engine of locomotion. Beneath this mass there lay a great quantity of dried grasses. The thought came to me that Robur was preparing to leave this retreat forever!

In fact, he could not be ignorant that the attention of the public was now keenly fixed upon the Great Eyrie; and that some further attempt was likely to be made to penetrate it. Must he not fear that some day or other the effort would be successful, and that men would end by invading his hiding place? Did he not wish that they should find there no single evidence of his occupation?

The sun disappeared behind the crests of the Blue Ridge. His rays now lighted only the very summit of Black Dome towering in the northwest. Probably the Terror awaited only the night in order to begin her flight. The world did not yet know that the automobile and boat could also transform itself into a flying machine. Until now, it had never been seen in the air. And would not this fourth transformation be carefully concealed, until the day when the Master of the World chose to put into execution his insensate menaces?

Toward nine o'clock profound obscurity enwrapped the hollow. Not a star looked down on us. Heavy clouds driven by a keen eastern wind covered the entire sky. The passage of the Terror would be invisible, not only in our immediate neighborhood, but probably across all the American territory and even the adjoining seas.

At this moment Turner, approaching the huge stack in the middle of the eyrie, set fire to the grass beneath.

The whole mass flared up at once. From the midst of a dense smoke, the roaring flames rose to a height which towered above the walls of the Great Eyrie. Once more the good folk of Morganton and Pleasant Garden would believe that the crater had reopened. These flames would announce to them another volcanic upheaval.

I watched the conflagration. I heard the roarings and cracklings, which filled the air. From the deck of the Terror, Robur watched it also.

Turner and his companion pushed back into the fire the fragments which the violence of the flames cast forth. Little by little the huge bonfire grew less. The flames sank down into a mere mass of burnt-out ashes; and once more all was silence and blackest night.

Suddenly I felt myself seized by the arm. Turner drew me toward the Terror. Resistance would have been useless. And moreover what could be worse than to be abandoned without resources in this prison whose walls I could not climb!

As soon as I set foot on the deck, Turner also embarked. His companion went forward to the look-out; Turner climbed down into the engine-room, lighted by electric bulbs, from which not a gleam escaped outside.

Robur himself was at the helm, the regulator within reach of his hand, so that he could control both our speed and our direction. As to me, I was forced to descend into my cabin, and the hatchway was fastened above me. During that night, as on that of our departure from Niagara, I was not allowed to watch the movements of the Terror.

Nevertheless, if I could see nothing of what was passing on board, I could hear the noises of the machinery. I had first the feeling that our craft, its bow slightly raised, lost contact with the earth. Some swerves and balancings in the air followed. Then the turbines underneath spun with prodigious rapidity, while the great wings beat with steady regularity.

Thus the Terror, probably forever, had left the Great Eyrie, and launched into the air as a ship launches into the waters. Our captain soared above the double chain of the Alleghenies, and without doubt he would remain in the upper zones of the air until he had left all the mountain region behind.

But in what direction would he turn? Would he pass in flight across the plains of North Carolina, seeking the Atlantic Ocean? Or would he head to the west to reach the Pacific? Perhaps he would seek, to the south, the waters of the Gulf of Mexico. When day came how should I recognize which sea we were upon, if the horizon of water and sky encircled us on every side?

Several hours passed; and how long they seemed to me! I made no effort to find forgetfulness in sleep. Wild and incoherent thoughts assailed me. I felt myself swept over worlds of imagination, as I was swept through space, by an aerial monster. At the speed which the Terror possessed, whither might I not be carried during this interminable night? I recalled the unbelievable voyage of the Albatross, of which the Weldon Institute had published an account, as described by Mr. Prudent and Mr. Evans. What Robur, the Conqueror, had done with his first airship, he could do even more readily with this quadruple machine.

At length the first rays of daylight brightened my cabin. Would I be permitted to go out now, to take my place upon the deck, as I had done upon Lake Erie?

I pushed upon the hatchway: it opened. I came half way out upon the deck.

All about was sky and sea. We floated in the air above an ocean, at a height which I judged to be about a thousand or twelve hundred feet. I could not see Robur, so he was probably in the engine room. Turner was at the helm, his companion on the look-out.

Now that I was upon the deck, I saw what I had not been able to see during our former nocturnal voyage, the action of those powerful wings which beat upon either side at the same time that the screws spun beneath the flanks of the machine.

By the position of the sun, as it slowly mounted from the horizon, I realized that we were advancing toward the south. Hence if this direction had not been changed during the night this was the Gulf of Mexico which lay beneath us.

A hot day was announced by the heavy livid clouds which clung to the horizon. These warnings of a coming storm did not escape the eye of Robur when toward eight o'clock he came on deck and took Turner's place at the helm. Perhaps the cloud bank recalled to him the waterspout in which the Albatross had so nearly been destroyed, or the mighty cyclone from which he had escaped only as if by a miracle above the Antarctic Sea.

It is true that the forces of Nature which had been too strong for the Albatross, might easily be evaded by this lighter and more versatile machine. It could abandon the sky where the elements were in battle and descend to the surface of the sea; and if the waves beat against it there too heavily, it would always find calm in the tranquil depths.

Doubtless, however, there were some signs by which Robur, who must be experienced in judging, decided that the storm would not burst until the next day.

He continued his flight; and in the afternoon, when we settled down upon the surface of the sea, there was not a sign of bad weather. The Terror is a sea bird, an albatross or frigate bird, which can rest at will upon the waves! Only we have this advantage, that fatigue has never any hold upon this metal organism, driven by the inexhaustible electricity!

The whole vast ocean around us was empty. Not a sail nor a trail of smoke was visible even on the limits of the horizon. Hence our passage through the clouds had not been seen and signaled ahead.

The afternoon was not marked by any incident. The Terror advanced at easy speed. What her captain intended to do I could not guess. If he continued in this direction, we should reach some one of the West Indies, or beyond that, at the end of the Gulf, the shore of Venezuela or Colombia. But when night came, perhaps we would again rise in the air to clear the mountainous barrier of Guatemala and Nicaragua, and take flight toward Island X, somewhere in the unknown regions of the Pacific.

Evening came. The sun sank in a horizon red as blood. The sea glistened around the Terror, which seemed to raise a shower of sparks in its passage. There was a storm at hand. Evidently our captain thought so. Instead of being allowed to remain on deck, I was compelled to re-enter my cabin, and the hatchway was closed above me.

In a few moments from the noises that followed, I knew that the machine was about to be submerged. In fact, five minutes later, we were moving peacefully forward through the ocean's depths.

Thoroughly worn out, less by fatigue than by excitement and anxious thought, I fell into a profound sleep, natural this time and not provoked by any soporific drug. When I awoke, after a length of time which I could not reckon, the Terror had not yet returned to the surface of the sea.

This maneuver was executed a little later. The daylight pierced my porthole; and at the same moment I felt the pitching and tossing to which we were subjected by a heavy sea.

I was allowed to take my place once more outside the hatchway; where my first thought was for the weather. A storm was approaching from the northwest. Vivid lightning darted amid the dense, black clouds. Already we could hear the rumbling of thunder echoing continuously through space. I was surprised—more than surprised, frightened! —by the rapidity with which the storm rushed upward toward the zenith. Scarcely would a ship have had time to furl her sails to escape the shock of the blast, before it was upon her! The advance was as swift as it was terrible.

Suddenly the wind was unchained with unheard of violence, as if it had suddenly burst from this prison of cloud. In an instant a frightful sea uprose. The breaking waves, foaming along all their crests, swept with their full weight over the Terror. If I had not been wedged solidly against the rail, I should have been swept overboard!

There was but one thing to do—to change our machine again into a submarine. It would find security and calm at a few dozen feet beneath the surface. To continue to brave the fury of this outrageous sea was impossible.

Robur himself was on deck, and I awaited the order to return to my cabin—an order which was not given. There was not even any preparation for the plunge. With an eye more burning than ever, impassive before this frightful storm, the captain looked it full in the face, as if to defy it, knowing that he had nothing to fear.

It was imperative that the Terror should plunge below without losing a moment. Yet Robur seemed to have no thought of doing so. No! He preserved his haughty attitude as of a man who in his immeasurable pride, believed himself above, or beyond humanity.

Seeing him thus I asked myself, with almost superstitious awe, if he were not indeed a demoniac being, escaped from some supernatural world.

A cry leaped from his mouth, and was heard amid the shrieks of the tempest and the howlings of the thunder. "I, Robur! Robur!— The Master of the World!"

He made a gesture which Turner and his companions understood. It was a command; and without any hesitation these unhappy men, insane as their master, obeyed it.

The great wings shot out, and the airship rose as it had risen above the falls of Niagara. But if on that day it had escaped the might of the cataract, this time it was amidst the might of the hurricane that we attempted our insensate flight.

The airship soared upward into the heart of the sky, amid a thousand lightning flashes, surrounded and shaken by the bursts of thunder. It steered amid the blinding, darting lights, courting destruction at every instant.

Robur's position and attitude did not change. With one hand on the helm, the other on the speed regulator, while the great wings beat furiously, he headed his machine toward the very center of the storm, where the electric flashes were leaping from cloud to cloud.

I must throw myself upon this madman to prevent him from driving his machine into the very middle of this aerial furnace! I must compel him to descend, to seek beneath the waters a safety which was no longer possible, either upon the surface of the sea or in the sky! Beneath, we could wait until this frightful outburst of the elements was at an end!

Then amid this wild excitement my own passions, all my instincts of duty, arose within me! Yes, this was madness! Yet must I not arrest this criminal whom my country had outlawed, who threatened the entire world with his terrible invention? Must I not put my hand on his shoulder and summon him to surrender to justice! Was I or was I not Strock, chief inspector of the federal police? Forgetting where I was, one against three, uplifted in mid-sky above a howling ocean, I leaped toward the stern, and in a voice which rose above the tempest, I cried as I hurled myself upon Robur:

"In the name of the law, I—"

Suddenly the Terror trembled as if from a violent shock. All her frame quivered, as the human frame quivers under the electric fluid. Struck by the lightning in the very middle of her powerful batteries, the airship spread out on all sides and went to pieces.

With her wings fallen, her screws broken, with bolt after bolt of lightning darting amid her ruins, the Terror fell from a height of more than a thousand feet into the ocean beneath.

Chapter 18

The Old Housekeeper's Last Comment

When I came to myself, after having been unconscious for many hours, a group of sailors whose care had restored me to life surrounded the door of a cabin in which I lay. By my pillow sat an officer who questioned me; and as my senses slowly returned, I answered to his questioning.

I told them everything. Yes, everything! And assuredly my listeners must have thought that they had upon their hands an unfortunate whose reason had not returned with his consciousness.

I was on board the steamer *Ottawa*, in the Gulf of Mexico, headed for the port of New Orleans. This ship, while flying before the same terrific thunderstorm which destroyed the Terror, had encountered some wreckage among whose fragments was entangled my helpless body.

Thus I found myself back among humankind once more, while Robur the Conqueror and his two companions had ended their adventurous careers in the waters of the Gulf. The Master of the World had disappeared forever, struck down by those thunderbolts which he had dared to brave in the regions of their fullest power. He carried with him the secret of his extraordinary machine.

Five days later the *Ottawa* sighted the shores of Louisiana; and on the morning of the tenth of August she reached her port. After taking a warm leave of my rescuers, I set out at once by train for Washington, which more than once I had despaired of ever seeing again.

I went first of all to the bureau of police, meaning to make my earliest appearance before Mr. Ward.

What was the surprise, the stupefaction, and also the joy of my chief, when the door of his cabinet opened before me! Had he not every reason to believe, from the report of my companions, that I had perished in the waters of Lake Erie?

I informed him of all my experiences since I had disappeared, the pursuit of the destroyers on the lake, the soaring of the Terror from amid

Niagara Falls, the halt within the crater of the Great Eyrie, and the catastrophe, during the storm, above the Gulf of Mexico.

He learned for the first time that the machine created by the genius of this Robur, could traverse space, as it did the earth and the sea.

In truth, did not the possession of so complete and marvelous a machine justify the name of Master of the World, which Robur had taken to himself? Certain it is that the comfort and even the lives of the public must have been forever in danger from him; and that all methods of defense must have been feeble and ineffective.

But the pride which I had seen rising bit by bit within the heart of this prodigious man had driven him to give equal battle to the most terrible of all the elements. It was a miracle that I had escaped safe and sound from that frightful catastrophe.

Mr. Ward could scarcely believe my story. "Well, my dear Strock," said he at last, "you have come back; and that is the main thing. Next to this notorious Robur, you will be the man of the hour. I hope that your head will not be turned with vanity, like that of this crazy inventor!"

"No, Mr. Ward," I responded, "but you will agree with me that never was inquisitive man put to greater straits to satisfy his curiosity."

"I agree, Strock; and the mysteries of the Great Eyrie, the transformations of the Terror, you have discovered them! But unfortunately, the still greater secrets of this Master of the World have perished with him."

The same evening the newspapers published an account of my adventures, the truthfulness of which could not be doubted. Then, as Mr. Ward had prophesied, I was the man of the hour.

One of the papers said, "Thanks to Inspector Strock, the American police still lead the world. While others have accomplished their work, with more or less success, by land and by sea, the American police hurl themselves in pursuit of criminals through the depths of lakes and oceans and even through the sky."

Yet, in following, as I have told, in pursuit of the Terror, had I done anything more than by the close of the present century will have become the regular duty of my successors?

It is easy to imagine what a welcome my old housekeeper gave me when I entered my house in Long Street. When my apparition—does not the word seem just—stood before her, I feared for a moment she would drop dead, poor woman! Then, after hearing my story, with eyes streaming with tears, she thanked Providence for having saved me from so many perils.

"Now, sir," said she, "now—was I wrong?"

"Wrong? About what?"

"In saying that the Great Eyrie was the home of the devil?"

"Nonsense; this Robur was not the devil!"

"Ah, well!" replied the old woman, "he was worthy of being so!"